ROOM 225-6

ROOM 225-6

A novel
by Karsten Schubert

Ridinghouse

For ████████████

'I am not I: thou art not he or she:
they are not they.'

Evelyn Waugh
Brideshead Revisited (1945)

'DUMB BRITAIN
National Lottery – In It To Win It, BBC 1

Dale Winton: What was the English composer Elgar's
first name?
Contestant: Wolfgang.'

Private Eye, no.1369, June 2014

1

[Editorial note: The first half of this book was mainly concerned with the author's stay at the Royal Brompton Hospital, where he had undergone major cancer surgery. A total thyroidectomy with selective dissection of cervical lymph nodes was performed with great success by two surgeons, Peter and Simon. Chapter One was full of medical jargon which the author had picked up during his five days on the ward. We had it read by a number of professionals, and their reports all stated pretty much the same: that the text was confused, half understood and would need major revision. Some doctors suggested that the chapter was beyond rescue and should be excised altogether. 'Half-baked' and 'ignorant' were the words that were used with monotonous regularity. The term 'bullshit' came up seven times (in four reports). Editorial here at Ridinghouse thought that the chapter was boring. A huge fight ensued. We won. So the book is now mainly about the aftermath of the author's hospital stay. For recuperation he moved into a suite at Claridge's (courtesy of two deluded 'friends' of his) and stayed there from June 11 until the end of the month. The author was not gracious about losing the battle and stormed out of a subsequent how-to-move-forward meeting at Ridinghouse, leaving behind a pile of barely intelligible notes stuffed into a Claridge's laundry bag and his laptop. This material the editorial team transcribed and put into some sort of chronological order (none of the notes were dated). To this we added the few funny bits we were able to rescue from Chapter One. There was not much worth saving. We also included a few chatty emails we found on the author's laptop (again there were not many). As for the veracity of the material included we are sure that most of the events will have taken place, though it must be admitted that the author has a reputation for exaggeration, and they may not have happened quite in the sequence here set out. We followed advice from Legal and redacted a number of names. When we showed the author the resulting manuscript he was delighted but said that the editorial note should be removed. Another huge fight ensued. We won again.]

[Excerpt from an email to Lynne]
The operation took 8½ hours and was performed by two surgeons in tandem, one (Simon) who sawed through my collarbone so that the other (Peter) could take a good look behind. The preparatory work (tests, scans, X-rays, consultations, blood work etc, etc) took place at three different London sites, allowing me to turn into an expert in twentieth-century hospital architecture (possible sequel to *The Curator's Egg*? I am in preliminary talks with Ridinghouse).

What comes out in the pre-operation investigations is that I have medullary cancer, which is one of the rarer forms of thyroid cancer and slightly harder to treat: there is the prospect of six weeks of radiation, not guaranteed but definitely a looming possibility.

The hospital stay was very uneventful, the boredom punctuated by medical stuff, inevitably more gruesome in anticipation than reality. There was only one truly horrid episode, but I will spare you the gory details. I could not concentrate on anything really, so I spent my time watching every episode of *House of Cards* with Kevin Spacey.

After the operation I have taken the doctors by surprise

and recovered much faster than expected, considering the scale of the intervention. At no point have I felt pain and I am now virtually off the painkillers. This is probably the only time I ever felt truly grateful for my solid German genes. The post-op analysis was very encouraging, the biopsy showed nothing new. You learn very quickly in this game that the best news is affirmation of what has already been suspected or actually confirmed. Finding less is unsettling (because – what else have they not found?) and finding more is definitely BAD news. You grade cancers by proliferation rate, expressed as a percentage figure: 0% is no cancer, and 100% the fastest shit you can possibly get. Mine turns out to be a snoozing puppy at 10%, which is great on two counts: If anything is left inside me (which is what we are in the midst of trying to establish) at least I don't need to clamber into the nearest ambulance and screech to a hospital NOW to beat the proliferation rate. We can take our time and be thorough (though believe me I want this over and done with ASAP). On the downside this slow growth explains why nobody (including me) ever picked up on what was going on: the beast grew so slow that it escaped detection, for three if not four years! I could not tell. I never had a before-and-after comparison of the kind you would have within weeks at 100% proliferation: one day you feel fine and a month later you are swollen up with cancer. For example I never noticed how restricted my breathing had become, but after the operation I am constantly taken aback at the ease with which I can fill my lungs with oxygen – it feels rather sensational. The cancer gradually had pushed my windpipe sideways, slowly choking me, a bit like a boa strangling a rabbit, but in extremely slow motion.

All this has been sorted out privately, and the medical bills are flooding in daily. If they had a proliferation rate it would be closer to 100%. This is the first time in my life having money made really meaningful sense to me. As for not detecting things, only with hindsight does everybody agree that my neck had begun to look fat. Now I actually look like I had some very expensive cosmetic surgery, you know the type they talk about in *Vogue*, very discreet, invisible yet not completely, definitely detectable to those in the know, like a very expensive logo-free handbag.

Five days after the operation I am allowed to leave the hospital.

2

My recollections of the first few days at Claridge's are a little hazy. I am still on painkillers, and they make you very woozy. They also give you terrible constipation, but that is another story. Oddly enough, despite the medication I am still in pain, mainly from my back; lying down and getting up is difficult. The Scar is healing well but looks very scabby. It has a slightly yellow-purple-green halo. Some areas of The Scar are oozing a brownish liquid, something between blood and pus, and this makes the front of my shirts look very unappetising, as if I suffer a bad cold and routinely blow my nose with my shirt-front.

I am not very good at doing nothing, so I spend my time exploring the neighbourhood, emailing and socialising. Especially socialising: I entertain people for lunch, tea and breakfast, often back-to-back. Doro is keeping my social diary, but she gets fed up with the whole business after about five days. She finally tells me that she has better things to do, like running Ridinghouse – so could I please keep my own schedule? I try, and to my amazement it is actually not that difficult.

I love my suite. It has its own little entrance lobby, painted oxblood red, a sitting room with a marble fireplace, a small, round dining table that can seat up to six, a very comfortable sofa and armchairs, and a desk in front of the window. The bedroom has a king-size bed, three built-in wardrobe cupboards with floor-to-ceiling mirrors and a vanity table in front of the window. It all is exactly how I like it, slightly old-fashioned, but all of it has been given a careful update, just enough for it to not look fuddy-duddy. The bathroom is white marble with black trim, with a walk-in shower and a huge bathtub. The bathroom has frosted windows (I dislike hotel bathrooms without windows). My suite is overlooking Brook Mews at the back of Claridge's. It is quiet except for the truck collecting empty bottles from the service entrance of the hotel at about six o'clock every morning. As I am usually up by then it does not matter.

One of the wardrobes I have designated the present cupboard, and it quickly fills up with gifts that are arriving at an astounding rate. The office had emailed all my friends please not to send flowers but that I would appreciate bottles of Japanese whisky. People are very obliging. Other booze is arriving too: bottles of champagne and claret but also books, catalogues and DVDs; it never stops.

Before I arrived at the hotel from the hospital the office had moved some of my personal belongings there, not just clothes, but books, my laptop, a row of Egyptian ushabtis – death is clearly still very much on my mind – a small Egyptian schist torso, and a 1925 Neo-Classical Picasso portrait drawing of Enrico Cecchetti. He was the ballet master of La Scala, from where Diaghilev headhunted him to get the dancers of his Ballets Russes up to scratch. Cecchetti was not only a famous dancer in his own right but also a great teacher and the inventor of a particular method for training young dancers, still much in use today, the Cecchetti Method. In the hallway on one of the tables I place Michael Landy's blue pencil copy of Cézanne's *Large Bathers* at the National Gallery. I commissioned it from him four years ago when he became artist-in-residence at the NG. You can see it the moment you walk into the suite. On my bedside table sits a jam-jar full of beach glass, one of about thirty I have filled over the years walking along shorelines all over Europe and America; it calms me down. Don't ask. There are dark red peonies in the sitting room. It all looks very comfortable and at home.

Within a few days I have established a routine. My greatest anxiety during the first days is the thought of having to move out at the end. I come up with a plan for how to stay on: I could sell my home in Kentish Town – this would give me enough money to stay on at Claridge's for at least two years, though I would have to start shopping at Lidl, do my laundry by hand in the bathroom sink and prepare my meals in the bedroom on a hotplate carefully hidden at the back of the sock drawer. After two or so years I would of course run out of cash, but by then, I figure, I would be really chummy with management. I then pull a Duchess of Argyll and run up a huge tab. We all know of course how that ended at the Dorchester. They too will turf me out from here, but hopefully I will be too old and gaga by then to care or even notice. Thomas Adès could then write one of his late operatic masterpieces about me, the bookend to *Powder Her Face*. I could even contribute my own libretto and earn a few pennies! Anyway all this is far off in the future, and I caution myself not to get too worked up about it.

[Excerpt from an email to Lynne (continued)]
My daily routine is a bit like this:

5-ish am Up (very early, I guess I am just too elated about being alive to waste time sleeping).

Order breakfast (always the same, Darjeeling, lightly done white toast and apricot jam).

Bath and dressing (shallow bath – I am still worried about dissolving the stitches on my neck prematurely – and then what? It would be very messy and is not worth thinking about).

8 am Pilates, at my usual gym in Soho with my regular teacher, Cordelia. She has been amazing through all this drama. At first our sessions were more like therapy and there was very little Pilates, but over time we are getting back to my old routine.

10 am Office and collect The Bitch, my three-and-half-year-old border terrier, absolutely adorable. To begin with she stays with various people from the office overnight. I am not yet up to a late-night walk through Mayfair, and a little nervous about embarrassing incidents on the hotel carpet. To begin with I last for about an hour at the office and leave completely exhausted. I find concentrating very hard. From the day of diagnosis everybody at the office has been extremely helpful. I have been protected from day-to-day crap with great efficiency. I wish it could carry on like this for ever. Of course it won't.

Walking The Bitch in Green Park. She loves it.

11-ish I meet with a hotel staff member in suite to discuss the day, plan lunch, tea and dinner menus, etc.

12.30 pm Lunch.

2 pm Nap.

3 to 6 pm (most days) Tea. Yesterday we were about 25, with tea, sandwiches, cakes and champagne.

6–7 pm Another nap.

8 pm Dinner (not every evening – I have started going out).

Hard traffic and carpets may be worn through by the time I am done.

I have always wondered why a certain type of socialite looks so strained and worn out. Now I know from personal experience. THEY ARE WORKING INCREDIBLY HARD ALL THE TIME AND IT IS UNBELIEVABLY EXHAUSTING. The attention to detail required is an absolute killer and it never lets off. I feel I am morphing into Brooke Astor. Mercifully the proliferation rate is so low (less than 5% maybe) that not much will have happened by the time I move out of here. I also have a feeling that Brooke Astor may have been much more laid back than her German doppelgänger. Positively sloppy, actually.

   It is very easy to fall into the rhythm and tone of the place. Because there is nothing to fault in general, unless you are a complete unreasonable prick, you start obsessing about minutiae; things that really should not matter at all but suddenly take on importance quite out of proportion to their reality. For example I DETEST SERVING TROLLEYS – I really don't know where this is coming from or why – and PREFER TRAYS. Another pet peeve is that NOBODY UNDERSTANDS HOW TO FOLD THE DOG BLANKET PROPERLY. I always HAVE TO DO IT AGAIN after the maid has left the room. Another big problem is that the hotel DOES NOT KNOW HOW TO DO FLOWERS, so I have to do it myself. Thank God there is a very adorable flower shop on Davies Street and they cater to all my needs. In the morning before I leave the room I have to rush about, gather laundry for collection, attend to the present wardrobe, sort piles of books and put notices in strategic places: DO NOT TOUCH this or that, or FLOWERS NEED FRESH WATER, or DO NOT MOVE BLANKET, or PLEASE REMOVE EXTRA CHAIR, or ADD DINING

CHAIR. It never ends. Real breakthrough this morning when I called room service, the guy WITHOUT PROMPTING said that he would bring my tea ON A TRAY. All this is helped by my being extra friendly to every staff member I come into contact with. I don't think that they are being shown much love by too many guests, so a little politeness gets you miles ahead. A bowl of two-pound coins from which I distribute like confetti helps too. As a result everybody here treats me and The Bitch like royalty. Yesterday I threw my first completely unreasonable wobble when the footman set the dining table WITH THE WRONG TYPE OF WATER GLASSES. He looked at me as if I had completely lost my mind (which I had). I felt ashamed and tipped him double.

In case you were wondering who is paying for all this, I assure you that it is not me. ▬▬▬▬▬ is treating me to the suite and Ivor to the extras. As you can tell, I am in the midst of a truly epic attempt at maxing out his credit card. I don't know what he had thought would happen when he made his generous offer. Maybe he was imagining two weeks of chicken broth and some Vichy water as I floated about my suite in slippers and pyjamas, looking frail and drawn? He sure did not expect that the entire London art world would be in and out of that suite at his expense for three weeks. Ivor luckily is not only extremely generous but also very rich. Don't get me wrong here: I think generous and poor is OK too, but it just doesn't work so well. My friends sure spoil me. Between the suite and the extras enough money is being spent to keep a small African dictatorship in nuclear arms. Which spookily takes us back to proliferation rates in this email for the fourth time.

I shudder at the thought of reality and can see myself furtively fumbling for non-existent call-buttons by my

bedside back in Kentish Town. Thankfully I will be back
in the real world just in time before I become a monster.
[Editor: 'become'?]

It is this correspondence by the way which set off the whole
idea of a book. Lynne replied that she thought that my emails
about my illness and recuperation were very funny and egged
me on: what about turning it all into a novel? Had I not long
been looking for an excuse to write another book? She was
right of course but she obviously had no idea what she
was triggering. I tried to take my revenge a fortnight later by
manipulating her into agreeing to write a straight-faced
afterword. Lynne deftly deflected this by saying that my
writing was clear enough and did not need further explanation.
Flattery clearly gets her everywhere. Whichever way you look
at it, Lynne is to blame. There was an earlier, idle idea about
writing a book about my illness, a few days after the initial
diagnosis, but I had dismissed the notion quickly. The last thing
the world needed, I had thought, was another generic cancer
memoir: just take a look on Amazon.

Once the idea of the novel was planted in my head things
progressed fast. Oddly enough the first thing that occurred to
me was the title and a mental image of the cover. The cover
you see is exactly as I imagined it from the beginning, except
for the Dolly Parton image on the back – that is a later addition.
I described what I had in mind to the designer, Tim, and he got
it exactly right. Marketing thought that the title could be snappier,
say *Room 225*, but I couldn't agree, I didn't want anyone to
think that I only had a single room, not a suite. As for the type
of writing I had in mind, I was hoping for something akin to The
Bitch's saunter, quick, confident and funny. I collected notes all
through my stay at the hotel, and work on the manuscript
started the moment Lynne had raised the idea. I handed the
finished manuscript to the editor ten weeks later.

The entire cancer episode has done something strange to my sense of time. It is not that time appears shorter or longer. I can no longer tell the speed at which an event is moving, and the moment an episode has passed it feels instantly like a very long time ago. Only a week or two afterwards even the surgery felt distant – I am talking years rather than days or months. Everything takes on a strange equidistant quality. It is both unnerving and reassuring at the same time.

Time dissolves. To begin with narrative and narrated time, fact and fiction, now and then, lose all their demarcations. Time at the hospital, time at the hotel, recovery time, party time, telling stories and told stories, past and present and future, it all becomes an amorphous one. Only gradually, as the story takes shape on paper, with fact and invention weaving in and out of the manuscript, and as the idea of the novel gradually solidifies into a proper typescript that no longer requires invention but solid craft (and the hand of an experienced literary editor), not the deft outline brushstroke of impressions but careful attention to every individual sentence, to make each ring and sound right and the whole chime as one, only then does my concept of time gradually come back to normal, 'normal' in the sense it unfolded before illness and recovery took over, before the events narrated and invented in here, 'normal' in the sense of a day-by-day, hour-by-hour progression, at the pace of a clock, predictable, reliable and just a little boring.

As 'normal' returns I even feel a little disappointed, as if something has been taken away from me, or as if I had become addicted to the high-pitched state of emergency that has become my life. Of course it could not carry on and it should not – it's physically and emotionally impossible. The high-octane craziness has to end at some point, and normal life has to resume, for my own sake and for the sake of the people around me. There is also another mechanism, complementary in a way to the one described above, which helps with this 'return to normal': conversations with other cancer sufferers are extremely helpful to turn the whole episode into 'normal'. In narrating and re-narrating the events from diagnosis onward, the story becomes more manageable, and as your delivery becomes honed in the repetition, what you are telling loses its rawness. If you are lucky you can after a while narrate the whole business with the verve of a stand-up comedian. Listening to others afflicted it becomes gradually clear that one's own experience is not singular at all but is shared by all with the same predicament. What struck you as the sheer mind-blowing uniqueness of your experience turns out to be extremely common and by and large shared by everybody in that situation. Comparing notes is immensely therapeutic and can be very funny. You can tell each other the most grisly detail and explode into hilarity, and it turns into a sort of game: who can fill in the most stomach-churning detail? It is like looking into a mirror. You are, after all, it turns out, not alone, and that is a huge relief. Sarah thought that the last sentence sounded like from a cancer memoir. Darling, this is a cancer memoir.

It is only six weeks from when I noticed the hard lump on my neck to my arrival at Claridge's. I had been to the opera with Doro and Sarah, to see Thomas Adès's *Powder Her Face*. There is not much interesting contemporary opera about, but this is definitely one of the best recent ones (this ENO production was to celebrate the twentieth anniversary of its premiere, hard to believe: Adès was 26 when he wrote it). I am tired, and at a traffic light on the way home I idly massage the left-hand side of my neck. There it suddenly is, a rock-hard lump, more like bone than tissue. It cannot have been there long, I would have noticed when shaving. Fuck, I think. At home I place myself in front of the bathroom mirror and take a really good look. You cannot see the lump, but you can feel it. But there is something much more disturbing: the base of my neck on the left side is definitely, massively swollen, and when I swallow I clearly have a goitre. Now that I am aware of this I cannot believe I never noticed it before. This is definitely not good. I keep touching and massaging the swelling and the lump, but they won't go away. If I hold my head in a particular way I can render both lump and goitre invisible, but it doesn't help much, it just looks as if I am holding my head in a funny and very uncomfortable way. Whatever this is, I think calmly, it is the last thing I need.

Rather than visiting my GP (whom I rarely see and barely know) I decide to wait till the upcoming Easter weekend. It so happens by sheer luck that I will have three doctors stay with me in Norfolk: Peter (a GP), Richard (a Consultant Paediatric Anaesthesiologist at Great Ormond Street) and Pauline (a Consultant Radiologist at King's College Hospital in south London). Pauline is visiting because we have an appointment to see The Bitch's breeders, a farmer and his wife outside Wisbech. Pauline's border terrier, Bowzer, died aged fifteen last year, and she is ready for a new dog. I cannot recommend 'my' breeders enough: they are wonderful people, kind and friendly and dedicated. They care about their dogs passionately, and I like to think of The Bitch as a prime product of this.

The next forty-eight hours are not easy, I keep fingering the goitre and the hard lump, and I make some gentle forays on Google. I have been told that if you have a medical problem the worst place to go to for information is the internet, because there is so much unreliable, unfiltered stuff on there, and without professional training how can you tell what is and what isn't true, but like everybody else I disregard this useful advice. I stick to the 'good' websites, like NHS Direct. My problem, it appears, is definitely my thyroid gland, and I pick out the diagnosis I find most comforting: I have, I tell myself, either an under- or over-function of my thyroid gland. This, the net reassures me, can be easily treated with medication.

I drive up to Norfolk very early on Saturday morning, to shop and prepare the house for the arrival of the doctors. The plan is to welcome my guests, show them their rooms, offer coffee or lunch and maybe a short walk on the beach followed by a nap. We will then light a fire in the sitting room and have tea morphing into drinks followed by dinner, for which I have bought two delicious free-range chickens and organic vegetables from the local farm shop. My plan is to broach the matter of my neck gently somehow late in the afternoon, to drop it in as a casual aside, as if I am hitting on a subject of not much interest and no consequence. Well, it doesn't quite pan out like this: their car has barely come to a standstill in the courtyard when I come shrieking out of the cottage towards them: DO ANY OF YOU KNOW ANYTHING ABOUT THYROID CONDITIONS?

They sit me down in the kitchen and in turn prod my neck. Now we all have been at the doctor's, and we have experienced that weird thing doctors do:

'Oh don't worry, this is nothing serious,' but you know that the doctor is actually worried too (just a little). Now imagine this multiplied by three: three doctors telling you like the chorus in a Greek tragedy that there is really nothing, absolutely nothing, to feel concerned about, the hard bit on my neck and the hugely swollen thyroid gland could be anything really, most likely nothing, but at the same time they are exchanging earnest, anxious glances that make me begin to fear that my life is quickly ebbing away. THEY ARE VERY WORRIED. Do they really think I am completely stupid and insensitive? I wonder. I mean there is obviously something critically amiss and they are seriously concerned – so why don't we cut the crap? I am not saying any of this, because I am not ready yet for the bad, hard news that is clearly beginning to take shape. At this stage I prefer the soft option, the unlikely diagnosis of a run-of-the-mill thyroid infection, 'nothing a course of antibiotics can't sort out'. Let's go with this for now.

So what next? We are having a perfunctory bit of tea and some toast, and then Pauline takes charge. She is a cool cat, I think, and just the kind of person you want to have around when there is a serious crisis afoot. I don't think much can faze her. There is no point speculating, she says, so why don't we just carry on as planned but leave Norfolk Sunday afternoon, and she will take me to King's on Monday morning to run a scan? And that's what we do. We have drinks and then dinner, and the evening is a great success, because by the end of it the four of us are completely plastered and can barely walk. On Sunday morning she and I are very nervous about the visit to the dog breeder, and we discuss the matter ad nauseam over breakfast. My anxiety is that the breeder might look at The Bitch and tell me to my face that I have ruined his dog. Pauline is worried that she might not pass muster and will not get onto the waiting list for a puppy. We talk about what to wear and which car to take in order to convey the right impression. What goes as country casual amongst country folk? Is the Land Rover OK, or does it look too London faux, or should we take Richard and Peter's BMW instead, or would this blow her chances? I think we are clinging to these irrelevant details because we really do not want to talk thyroid.

The dog breeder could not be sweeter. There are four bitches scampering about, two are pregnant. We agree that we will come back for a proper look two months later once the puppies have arrived. The farmer barely comments on The Bitch, and I am a little hurt, I mean at least he could say that she was pretty. Never mind. After this visit the doctors and I return to London.

The next morning Pauline, Peter and I head to King's for a

scan. It is Easter Monday, and the place is deserted. Walking into a hospital always makes my heart sink, but this time it feels bad to a different magnitude. On the diagnostic ward we end up in a curtained cubicle. Pauline lathers up my neck area with KY and begins the scan. I follow proceedings on a black-and-white TV monitor and to my mind things don't look too bad: there are a few dark bits, 'shadows' embedded in a lot of white or white-grey, and white is always good, right? I am sure that there is really nothing to worry about until Pauline explains that the white bits are actually the bad bits, the image comes up in negative. Holy cow! There is also something else: The screen is flecked with bits of white, like static. Now this is definitely a sign of something wrong. Still, the doctors are trying to keep up the illusion that all this could mean nothing, even though by then they are pretty emphatic that I will need an operation. GUYS, I AM NOT AN IDIOT, I want to say but I don't. I wipe my neck dry and put my shirt back on, and we head back to Pauline's home for a chat.

Over coffee they set out my options. They recommend two doctors who to their mind are the best in the thyroid field in Europe. Conveniently both are based in London. The second one they talk about makes most sense to me, he works embedded in a whole team – that is to say I will never have to get from one specialist to another on my own. Somebody will always be there for me. This sounds good.
'What is his name, and where is he based?'
'His name is Peter and he is at the Royal Marsden.'
Pauline checks herself quickly: 'Don't worry, just because he is at the national cancer hospital does not automatically mean that you have cancer, you know.'
Well, what else could it mean? She really thinks I am stupid. This is actually the first time that we have mentioned the C-word since Saturday. The three doctors and I have performed quite an elaborate avoidance dance over the last few days.

The following day Pauline refers me to Peter, and a meeting is set up for Wednesday evening. He is by all accounts an extremely busy man but somehow manages to squeeze in an extra appointment for me. I am his last patient for the day, at 6.30. I arrive with my friend Asun. She is kind, very intelligent and, above all, pretty unflappable. Just the kind of person you need to help digest the amount of scary information that is about to be thrown at you. The plan is that afterwards she will help me puzzle the whole thing together from what we can remember between us. I am literally shaking with fear, but not for long. Peter, it turns out, is not only one of the best doctors in his field; he is also brilliant at communicating with his patient. He reads me like an open book and calibrates what he is saying to my particular needs: where he senses nervousness or anxiety he goes into detail, when I am not worried he delivers the bare outline. What he is saying makes grim sense: I definitely have thyroid cancer. He can tell from reviewing the images we took on Easter Monday at King's College Hospital. He and I and his team will spend the next few weeks figuring out which particular type of thyroid cancer I actually have, followed by an operation and a hospital stay. More treatment, possibly or hopefully not, to follow later. I explain to him my biggest fear is not the cancer nor the operation nor the aftermath but my serious needle phobia. I feel a bit stupid bringing it up but there you are. Is there anything we could do? Valium, maybe? He promises to make a note of this and assures me that there will definitely be no problem on this front; the matter will be taken care off. In the end I will be prescribed Diazepam. It has taken care of my needle phobia ever since. As we leave the hospital I am in a strange state, not fear, not shock, just very matter-of-fact. I am amazed how calm I am.

Peter, I have already decided, will see me through this, as simple as that. I trust him. Everything will be fine.

3

After a few days it begins to feel like I have lived at the hotel for ever.

Breakfast. The morning order arrives. The first pot of tea comes ON A TRAY with twelve pieces of china. That is half a domestic dishwasher filled up efficiently.

The Bitch has finally moved in full-time and has taken to Claridge's like a duck to water. When we enter the lobby she likes to throw herself onto the cold marble floor so that I have to drag her by her lead to the lift. She can be so stubborn. Does she really have to embarrass me like this? I am not saying anything, as we are still trying to be friends again after my hospital episode. She felt neglected and would not even allow me to pet her for the first few days afterwards. She sure knows how to sulk.

Dinner parties in my suite are fun: I keep them small, never more than six, and simple: champagne, a salad starter and a main course, usually fish. It is asparagus season, so there is a lot of that. I choose some delicious claret, either from the stock in the present cupboard or from the hotel's extensive wine list. One of the first dinners is with Asun and Desmond, and Richard and GP-Peter, the two doctors – a sort of reunion of the original team. Pauline, unfortunately, can't join us. The conversation is mainly about medical stuff, but there are other topics as well. Everybody loves my suite. Asun talks about a three-part TV programme she watched a year or so ago about Claridge's. Had I seen it? She is not the first to mention this. As I do not own a TV I had missed it.

The next morning I have a word with Miles, the concierge. Would he have a recording of it I could borrow? In the afternoon a pageboy delivers a DVD to my room with a note:

> **For Room 225-6,**
> **As promised here is the DVD. Please return**
> **it to me when you are leaving us.**
> **With best wishes,**
> **Miles**

It is my 'evening off' so I watch the whole thing in one go on my laptop, sipping Japanese whisky and loving every minute. This is a truly post-modern moment, I think, sitting here in my suite watching a programme about the hotel I am staying in. Each of the three forty-five-minute episodes has a key scene.

In part one a female rock star is about to arrive with her entourage of thirty-five. She insists that the marble tub in her bathroom is replaced with a jacuzzi. No problem. The hotel prides itself for never saying no to customers. Ever. Without batting an eyelid the whole Claridge's machine switches into gear, and in four days the jacuzzi is installed. This involves a team of about eight plumbers and decorators. Judging by the number of people who mention it, the scene has become a sort of urban myth, and it is inevitably referred to as 'the business with Britney's jacuzzi'.

The second episode's set piece concerns the arrival of the Emperor and Empress of Japan. They turn up with an entourage of twenty-eight only, modest by comparison. It is all very grand and stately, but not exactly a surprise. I mean you would not expect them to stay at the Holiday Inn near Gatwick with self-catering, would you? Still, it makes for amazing TV.

The third episode is constructed around a Norwegian guy who forages for live ants. He sucks them up, one by one, with a straw if you can believe it, tens of thousands of the little critters, and delivers them to the kitchen at Claridge's to be served as a live hors d'oeuvre in their new pop-up restaurant. Even a third glass of whisky does not make this any more exciting, so I go back and I watch the jacuzzi and Emperor-and-Empress scenes again. I am stunned though at the Norwegian guy's endurance, I mean sucking up thousands of ants with a straw, one by one, takes some doing. Apparently the ants, in self-defence, spray the back of his throat with acid. Who can blame them?

The programme is pitch-perfect TV, *Downton Abbey* with room service, and at the centre stands the charming, committed hotel staff. Most of them seem to have worked at Claridge's for ever, and their dedication to the place is something to behold. They are loyal, unflappable and eternally cheerful. They truly love their customers. It is like a wonderful conspiracy everybody is in on, staff and guests alike: This is sheltered accommodation for rich, crazy people. I feel safe.

The star of the programme is undoubtedly Thomas, the forty-something German general manager. He is not only tall and photogenic, he also has the most impeccable sense of comic timing, perfect pitch and delivery. Every time he comes on you know you are in for a treat.

Compared with what I have just watched I am a model customer. My demands – aside from trays and a particular type of water glasses – are modest, if not plain boring. I am worried: am I a disappointment to the staff? Need I get my act together and come up with at least a few challenging ideas? I wonder.

I discover quickly that there is a question as to Britney's identity. She is never actually identified in the documentary, and the hotel won't say. Believe me I have tried, but they have closed ranks and are very discreet. There is a possibility that she is in fact a woman that is referred to as 'the Japanese Britney'.

There is also a 'German Britney' and a 'French Britney'. Every nation seems to have their own. This is no longer about a particular person but about an attitude. 'Doing a Britney' indicates generic rock-star behaviour of a certain, outlandish type. The actual Britney has merely set the benchmark everybody else is now aspiring to. If you think about it this is quite an achievement. Britney has become a metonym. Who Britney actually is has no bearing on how this novel will unfold. It is the thought that counts, not who thinks it.

Crossing the lobby on my way out the next morning I find a pound coin on the marble floor. I guess a pound in here is like a penny outside, so this must mean good luck. Things are looking up.

Tonight is the opening of Bridget Riley's exhibition at the David Zwirner Gallery. I have worked on this for a year, and I am determined not to miss the opening and dinner for anything, even if I am still weak and drugged up. Caroline has kindly offered to be my chaperon. Before we set off to the gallery we have a glass of champagne in my suite. We talk about politics, the ongoing fallout from the financial crisis, middle-class anxieties about being left behind. I point out to her that we maybe should not be drinking Krug from the minibar whilst discussing these topics. We get to the gallery, the place is rammed. People love the show. Bridget is happy. The dinner is a great success, and I leave exhausted after the main course. I can barely walk with pain.

The next day my old friend Sarah pays her first of many visits and joins me for lunch. Lunch is so late that she witnesses the setting up for the afternoon tea. A butler and a maid arrive with all the paraphernalia: there are two trolleys full of plates and tea cups, serving platters loaded with cucumber and smoked salmon sandwiches and The Cake, and on one of the chests of drawers are set up batteries of champagne flutes and ice buckets. Sarah is particularly intrigued by The Cake. What was the story?

I tell her. A cardboard box had been waiting for me on the dining table when I moved in five days ago. It came with a card that read:

With best wishes from all of us at the British Museum

The box contained a round marzipan-covered fruitcake, about eight inches in diameter. Printed on top, like a colour photograph, was an image of The Bitch. What a great gift! I called room service and asked them to take The Cake to the kitchen so that it could be kept refrigerated. Since then the cake has been up to the room every day for tea – but nobody, including me, has dared to cut it. Why, Sarah wants to know, has the BM sent me a cake? I tell her that they had sent it because they are my friends, but there is also another reason.

During the days after my diagnosis I was looking for ways to engineer a positive outcome. If I was to get through all this not just alive but also reasonably sane, what could I do to express my gratitude? I decided that if all turned out OK I would give the Department of Prints and Drawings a beautiful Degas drawing I had owned for many years. At age twenty the artist had visited Florence and made a number of copies after old master drawings he saw in the Uffizi. My drawing was one of these, a copy of a Ferrarese portrait of an aristocratic-looking man wearing a beret. But two days before my operation I realised what a shocking blunder I was about to make: you don't make deals with whatever higher authority you are appealing to. I was not only asking for trouble, I was asking for a rebuke and punishment. To get out of this predicament I quickly put the drawing in a plastic carrier and

sent it to the British Museum as an outright gift. Sarah is sceptical:
'Oh dear, I think you left it too late.'
'Sorry?'
'Well, God will see through your ruse right away.'
'There is nothing to see through. There is nothing here for God
to find fault with. It's an outright gift and there were no
conditions attached to it. None. None whatever.'
'I am not so sure.'
'What's that suppose to mean?'
'Well you know how God is: cruel and capricious.'
She can be such a pessimist. Personally I don't think there is
anything here God can possibly hold against me, though of
course she has managed to plant a nagging doubt.

I like to think of The Cake as a novel and elegant way to
express gratitude: you give the BM something not completely
uninteresting, and a week or so later a marzipan-covered fruit
cake, with a picture of your own dog on top, arrives in your
hotel suite. It's chic, personal and sentimental, and it sure beats
the usual black-tie thank-you dinner one gets invited to from
time to time. The Cake is truly special.

Anyway it is proffered at every tea party I hold but nobody
touches it. After five days I give up and put it on the side table
in my little entrance lobby. A few days later I look at it and it
has started expanding under the marzipan, the same way a
dead fish starts bloating. The marzipan is stretched to breaking
point. If it was a dead fish it would have exploded by now, with
internal organs and gut splashed everywhere. I take a knife to
the cake and lance the marzipan and the cake quietly deflates
back to its original shape.

I enthuse to Sarah about the quality of the hotel's service. It is
super efficient and feels as if the staff can read your mind. She
says that the reason for this is that Claridge's is only a glossier
version of that famous hotel in Moscow where all Westerners

had to stay during the Cold War. It all suddenly makes sense. There is actually a KGB station in the basement of Claridge's, and it is still running. The Russians, in the panic of 1989, had forgotten to shut it down. The station is now scraping a living by supplying hotel management with customer-service information. They really know everything.

Room service, breakfast order: 'Good morning. Could I please have a TRAY with a pot of Darjeeling, some toast and…uh…'
    'Apricot jam.'
'Yes please.'
    'Very well, sir.'
I think this is conclusive proof that the former KGB is running the whole show.

The Dog Blanket is of course, you may have realised by now, not the dog's blanket, but The Dog Blanket. It is sort of its name. I brought it with me from home, first to the hospital and now here. It is not particularly beautiful but a reminder of better times. It is comforting.

I am absolutely stunned when I walk into the bedroom and The Dog Blanket is GONE. Vanished. I am on the brink of fainting. It turns out that it has been moved from the bottom of the bed into one of the three closets. Needless to say IT IS FOLDED WRONG again. I am inclined to call Housekeeping to complain but I resist. Now I am writing a book it would be foolish to jeopardise the only interesting character in it. I mean if the blanket WAS ALWAYS IN THE SAME PLACE FOLDED EXACTLY AS IT SHOULD BE what would there be left to write about? Not much.

A few days in and I am getting a tad paranoid. Nothing serious, just a little nagging persecution mania triggered by the ennui of being looked after so well. I have problems with my mobile phone and outside callers seem to be unable to get through. The phone never rings. Are THEY systematically attempting to cut me off from the world? I will prepare a folded note that I will surreptitiously slip to my assistant, Antonio, on his next visit. (Keir thought that there were cameras in the wall lights on both sides of the fireplace. He would of course say this. Keir always presumes the worst – about anything.) The note will say:

I AM HELD AT CLARIDGE'S IN ROOM 225-6
AGAINST MY WILL.
PLEASE INFORM THE GERMAN EMBASSY
IN BELGRAVE SQUARE.

As Antonio is clever (and Spanish) he might trick THEM by heading to the Spanish Embassy (conveniently opposite the Germans) as if he was going to one of those parties these places throw for their own expats. This might fool THEM. Potential for an international incident, tense exchanges in the UN, etc, etc. Or not.

The second pot of tea arrives with EIGHT PIECES OF CHINA. Somebody has obviously read my previous note, and things are being stripped back so that I can no longer complain. Would it not be amusing to provoke THEM to the point that I will be served my tea on my last day here in a paper cup?

Mayfair from the outside is a different world than Mayfair from the inside. Claridge's seems to be the epicentre of it all. Every day, between 3 and 6, the lobby fills with exhausted shoppers ready to have tea. If you are not a hotel guest you will need to book this at least three months in advance. At this time of day the lobby looks more like a very upmarket refugee camp, everyone laden down with shopping bags. All the luxury brands are here, Chanel, Burberry, Victoria's Secret (not so luxurious, we will come to this later), Prada, Mulberry and Armani, except the jewellers. I never see a Graff Diamonds shopping bag – too dangerous, I guess. I will come to recognise the shoppers' facial expressions, a kind of jaded, disappointed glassy-eyed stare. Here is the rub: you may shop as hard as you like, but none of this shopping gives you any true satisfaction. You may be drawn to Bond Street for its exclusivity, but there are now so many rich people about that it feels as crowded as Oxford Street, only with bigger price tags. At certain hours it is gridlocked with Bentleys and SUVs with blacked-out windows, and bodyguards loiter in front of shopfronts, indistinguishable from the shops' own security guards in their dark suits and funny ear pieces. If anyone made a wrong move there could be a serious shoot-out.

There you are in pursuit of the latest must-have handbag or whats it, you finally get it, you beat all the hordes of fellow shoppers, bribe your way onto the waiting list for this or that item and pay a king's ransom, but in the end what you end up with is not a life-changer but just another handbag. And instead of learning the lesson and going home to start doing something rewarding, like reading a book or dispensing some charity work, you turn around and 'do' Bond Street in the opposite direction, in search of that elusive item. This time round, you promise yourself it will definitely redefine your life and make you happy. The argument is of course akin to the argument an alcoholic uses to justify his latest drink: this one will change it all and end the chain, but it never does. You have to be hard and harsh and glassy-eyed to keep up the illusion. So all the zombies carry on up and down Bond Street.

Most of the Bond Street traffic these days is either Chinese or Russian. The Chinese clearly enjoy themselves, chatting away and joking, while the majority of Russians just look glum and unsmiling. This must be the result of too much Botox, or maybe they are thinking about what their leader is up to right now, or it's both.

A day later, breakfast with Caroline, for a change in the foyer. We talk shop. The hotel does an amazing Japanese breakfast, a little bit of grilled salmon, white rice, a cold poached egg in vinegar, green tea, all served up on a red lacquer set. I feel sorry for Ivor's credit card. Caroline, unfortunately, ends up with half the egg down her ▬▬▬▬.
[This is a private joke between Caroline and the protagonist.]

Richard once said that my problem is that I am pathologically happy and that I should to talk to my GP to get medication for this. He may well be right. He comes for supper and we are having a wonderful time. We drink the first of twelve bottles of *Château Certan '88*. The wine is absolutely delicious. This is a mystery gift that arrived a few days ago, without a card or anything, and I have not yet figured out who it is from. All the obvious candidates deny it was them. Sarah's theory is, as always, the most amusing: that the wine was not for me but for a different room and was delivered in error. In case she is right I serve it every evening for dinner and the bottles are gone in four days.
[Author's note: I still have not found out who was so generous to me. In case it was you please drop me a line c/o Ridinghouse so that I can write a thank-you note.]

After dinner I take Richard downstairs to get a cab. The Bitch and I will have our evening walk. As we reach the lobby I realise that I forgot to bring a poo-bag. I ask the concierge if he could help out. He is trying his best and offers me a gold-embossed pale-green Claridge's miniature shopping bag with tassel handles and some silk wrapping paper. I decline the bag on the grounds that it is too beautiful to put a dog turd in, but take the paper. The Bitch and I are doing our usual loop round the neighbourhood. Mayfair at 10.30 pm is amazing, a sea of well-dressed, tipsy, roaring people. On Bond Street a number of shops are holding events for VIP shoppers, girls with clipboards eagerly screening out undesirables at the door. It is all very loud and self-confident and just a little bit nauseating, a moneyed freak show, to tell the truth. The Bitch and I end up on Berkeley Square. As we pass Annabel's The Bitch starts straining on her leash, trying to get to the staircase leading down to the club. A drunken man, holding himself up against the railing, is watching us glassy-eyed. He can barely stand up and reeks of booze.

'Lovely dog. What's his name?'
I tell him: 'She. She is a girl.'
The Bitch is virtually choking on her collar.

'Well, she wouldn't be the first bitch down there,' he says, swaying back into the railing.

The tea parties are a great success and easy to organise. I call people or email: 'Why don't you come for tea tomorrow, between three and six, Room 225-6?'

I don't even keep a record of whom I have invited, so the arrival of some guests and their particular combinations often comes as a surprise, and sometimes I feel like a guest at my own party. The room easily seats twelve. There will be tea, of course, champagne, sandwiches, scones, and The Cake. People admire it but nobody ever dares cutting into it. Maybe they do not want to destroy the image of The Bitch or maybe they find sheet marzipan disgusting. Anyway, all the other food is eaten without fail, all the champagne is drunk, but The Cake, day in day out, is taken back to the kitchen again, to be brought up again the following day for another try. What must they think in the kitchen? The parties are meant to be over by 6, but they usually run overtime, sometimes so late that the last guests leave when the butler has started laying the dinner table, and I miss my late afternoon nap. It is all a bit exhausting and out of control but still very enjoyable.

Over the days I see a great many people: Richard, Niamh, Ann-Marie and Spike, Frances, Sally, Jack, Maddy, Keir, Tom, Tess, another Frances, at least three Johns, Samia, Robin, Jane and Richard, Judith, Jack, Doro and Gavin, John and Virginia, Joseph, Angela, Kevin, Jeremy, Tim, Caroline, Sofia, Jake, Alison, Martin, Sally, Hugo, Duncan, Dylan, Diana and John, Paul, Desmond, Asun, Douglas, Tess, Gillian and Michael, Helen, Mandana, Nick, Penelope, Richard, Frankie, Julian and Felicity, Maureen, Alan, Norman, Bridget, James and Clare, Mandy, Penny, Vivienne, Achim, Francis, Robert and Gemma with their baby son Vaughan, Philip, Daniel, Anna, Louisa, another Robin, Stephen, Thomas, Marjorie. I love every minute of it. And it all becomes a blur.

The Scar is looking its most spectacular. If you are slightly short-sighted you might think that I am wearing a very rusty barbed-wire necklace that has gone a bit septic in places. Realising that it is just a scar must come as a relief.

The lobby is the centre of the Claridge's universe. It is arguably the most glamorous social space in central London. You enter through the revolving door, the foyer is in front of you, reception and lift on your left and the famous sweeping staircase on your right. It is all very theatrical, and people indeed cross the space as if they are acting the part of their own life in a stage play. On arrival I always take the lift up but when I come down I invariably use the staircase.

When coming down yesterday I passed Thomas, the general manager, and he smiled and nodded at me. Unfortunately he was on his mobile.

While one quickly begins to recognise faces of hotel staff members, says hello or nods at them with a smile, the fellow guests remain strangely anonymous. There is not even a glimmer of recognition when one passes in the lobby or corridors.

The only other guest I am really aware of is an elegant old lady with a white miniature poodle. The poodle and The Bitch nearly had a noisy fight in the lobby. The poodle was apoplectic with rage. He just lunged at The Bitch, unprovoked, out of the blue. What was he thinking? A poodle death wish? The old lady thought it was very funny. The Bitch hates small dogs. I assure you The Bitch is not a racist. Race is not her problem; it's size. The lady and the poodle are in a room diagonally opposite 225-6. Every time we walk past The Bitch bristles and snorts with derision. She is patient. One day the door will open and the poodle will prance out innocently. The poor mutt has no idea what he is in for.

Dylan comes for tea in my suite. He brings me as a gift another bottle of Japanese whisky. At this rate we will shortly run out of storage space. He is a lovely man, and I am fond of him, but ever since my medical trouble began I have found him a little tedious. Here is why. He is in the midst of a major medical situation himself, involving his ▮▮▮▮▮▮▮▮ and ▮▮▮▮▮▮▮▮. When we get together now we no longer animatedly talk about art or politics or whatever topic it may be. Instead he incessantly talks about his medical stuff, and I talk incessantly about mine. He isn't really listening to me, and I am most definitely not listening to him.

Now it is getting a little complicated, so please pay close attention. What I wanted to follow here was to show the same passage of a conversation with Dylan twice. The first version would have shown what Dylan was actually hearing of the conversation, the second version would have been what I heard.

If you read the two texts in tandem you might glean the odd, interesting insight into similarities and dissimilarities between medullary cancer and ████████████ and ████████████.
I know that the chances of this are minimal as this is strictly speaking not a 'conversation' but two spliced monologues, but still there might be the odd random insight that could amuse the more scientific-minded reader. Here we go.

What Dylan is hearing:

Protagonist: Blab bla blab bla bla bla blab bla blab la blab bla blab bla blab bla bla bla blab bla blab la blab bla bla blab bla blab bla blab la blab bla bla bla blab bla bla bla blab bla blab la blab bla blab bla bla bla blab bla blab la blab bla blab bla blab bla bla.

Dylan: ████████████████████████████████████
████████████████████████████████████
████████████████████████████████████
████████████████████████████████████
█████████████████████████.

Protagonist: Blab bla blab bla bla bla blab bla blab la blab bla blab bla blab bla bla bla blab bla blab la blab bla bla blab bla bla bla blab bla blab la blab bla bla bla blab bla bla bla blab bla la blab bla blab bla blab bla bla bla blab bla blab la blab bla blab bla blab bla.

Dylan: ████████████████████████████████████
████████████████████████████████████
████████████████████████████████████
████████████████████████████████████
█████████████████████████.

42

Protagonist: Blab bla blab bla bla bla blab bla blab la
blab bla blab bla bla bla blab bla blab la blab bla bla blab bla bla
bla blab bla blab la blab bla bla bla blab bla bla bla blab bla
la blab bla blab bla blab bla bla bla blab bla blab la blab bla blab
bla blab.

Dylan: ▬▬▬▬▬▬▬▬▬▬▬▬▬▬
▬▬▬▬▬▬▬▬▬▬▬▬▬
▬▬▬▬▬▬▬▬▬▬▬▬▬▬
▬▬▬▬▬▬▬▬▬▬▬▬▬▬
▬▬▬▬▬▬▬.

Protagonist: Blab bla blab bla bla bla blab bla blab la blab bla
blab bla blab bla bla bla blab bla blab la blab bla bla blab bla
bla blab bla blab la blab bla bla bla blab bla bla bla blab bla blab
la blab bla blab bla blab bla bla bla blab bla blab la blab
bla blab bla bla bla blab.

Dylan: ▬▬▬▬▬▬▬▬▬▬▬▬▬▬
▬▬▬▬▬▬▬▬▬▬▬▬▬
▬▬▬▬▬▬▬▬▬▬▬▬▬▬
▬▬▬▬▬▬▬▬▬▬▬▬▬▬
▬▬▬▬▬▬▬.

Protagonist: Blab bla blab bla bla bla blab bla blab la blab bla
blab bla blab bla bla bla blab bla blab la blab bla bla blab bla bla
bla blab bla blab la blab bla bla bla blab bla bla bla blab bla blab
la blab bla blab bla blab bla bla bla blab bla blab la blab bla blab
bla blab bla bla bla blab bla blab bla bla bla blab bla blab bla bla
bla blab bla blab bla bla bla blab.

Dylan: ▬▬▬▬▬▬▬▬▬▬▬▬▬▬
▬▬▬▬▬▬▬▬▬▬▬▬▬▬
▬▬▬▬▬▬▬▬▬▬▬▬▬▬

[REDACTED]

Protagonist: Blab bla blab bla bla bla blab bla blab la blab bla blab bla blab bla bla bla blab bla blab la blab bla bla blab bla bla bla blab bla blab la blab bla bla bla blab bla bla bla blab bla blab la blab bla blab bla blab bla bla bla blab bla blab la blab bla blab bla blab bla bla bla blab bla blab bla bla bla blab bla blab bla.

Dylan: [REDACTED]

Protagonist: Blab bla blab bla bla bla blab bla blab la blab bla blab bla blab bla bla bla blab bla blab la blab bla bla blab bla bla bla blab bla blab la blab bla bla bla blab bla bla bla blab bla blab la blab bla blab bla bla bla blab bla blab la blab bla blab bla blab bla bla bla blab bla blab bla bla bla.

Dylan: [REDACTED]

Protagonist: Blab bla blab bla bla bla blab bla blab la blab bla blab bla blab bla bla bla blab bla blab la blab bla bla blab bla bla bla blab bla blab la blab bla bla bla blab bla bla bla blab bla blab la blab bla blab bla bla bla blab bla blab la blab bla blab bla bla bla blab bla blab la blab bla bla blab bla bla bla blab bla blab la blab bla bblab bla blab bla bla bla blab bla blab la blab bla.

44

Dylan: ▓▓▓▓▓▓▓▓▓▓▓▓▓▓▓▓▓▓▓▓▓▓▓▓▓▓▓
▓▓▓▓▓▓▓▓▓▓▓▓▓▓▓▓▓▓▓▓▓▓▓▓▓▓▓
▓▓▓▓▓▓▓▓▓▓▓▓▓▓▓▓▓▓▓▓▓▓▓▓▓▓▓▓
▓▓▓▓▓▓▓▓▓▓▓▓▓▓▓▓▓▓▓▓▓▓▓▓▓
▓▓▓▓▓▓▓▓▓▓▓▓▓▓▓.

Protagonist: Blab bla blab bla bla bla blab bla blab la blab bla blab bla blab bla bla bla blab bla blab la blab bla bla blab bla bla bla blab bla blab la blab bla bla bla blab bla bla bla blab bla blab la blab bla blab bla blab bla bla bla blab bla blab la blab bla blab bla blab bla bla bla blab.

Dylan: ▓▓▓▓▓▓▓▓▓▓▓▓▓▓▓▓▓▓▓▓▓▓▓▓▓▓
▓▓▓▓▓▓▓▓▓▓▓▓▓▓▓▓▓▓▓▓▓▓▓▓▓▓
▓▓▓▓▓▓▓▓▓▓▓▓▓▓▓▓▓▓▓▓▓▓▓▓▓▓▓
▓▓▓▓▓▓▓▓▓▓▓▓▓▓▓▓▓▓▓▓▓▓▓▓▓
▓▓▓▓▓▓▓▓▓▓▓▓▓.

Protagonist: Blab bla blab bla bla bla blab bla blab la blab bla blab bla blab bla bla bla blab bla blab la blab bla bla blab bla bla bla blab bla blab la blab bla bla bla blab bla bla bla blab bla blab la blab bla blab bla blab bla bla bla blab bla blab la blab bla blab bla blab bla bla bla blab bla bla bla blab bla blab la blab bla bla blab bla bla bla blab bla blab la blab bla bblab bla blab bla bla bla blab bla blab la blab bla.

Dylan: ▓▓▓▓▓▓▓▓▓▓▓▓▓▓▓▓▓▓▓▓▓▓▓▓▓▓
▓▓▓▓▓▓▓▓▓▓▓▓▓▓▓▓▓▓▓▓▓▓▓▓▓
▓▓▓▓▓▓▓▓▓▓▓▓▓▓▓▓▓▓▓▓▓▓▓▓▓▓
▓▓▓▓▓▓▓▓▓▓▓▓▓▓▓▓▓▓▓▓▓▓▓▓▓▓
▓▓▓▓▓▓▓▓▓▓▓▓▓▓▓▓▓▓▓▓▓▓▓▓▓▓
▓▓▓▓.

Protagonist: Blab bla blab bla bla bla blab bla blab la blab bla blab bla blab bla bla bla blab bla blab la blab bla bla blab bla bla bla.

Dylan: ▓▓▓▓▓▓▓▓▓▓▓▓▓▓▓▓▓▓▓▓▓▓▓▓▓▓▓▓▓▓▓▓▓▓▓▓▓▓▓ ▓▓▓▓▓▓▓▓▓▓▓▓▓▓▓▓▓▓▓▓▓▓▓▓▓▓▓▓▓▓▓▓▓▓▓▓.

Protagonist: Blab bla blab bla bla bla blab bla blab la blab bla blab bla blab bla bla bla blab bla blab la blab bla bla blab bla bla bla blab bla blab la blab bla bla bla blab bla bla bla blab bla.

Dylan: ▓▓▓▓▓▓▓▓▓▓▓▓▓▓▓▓▓▓▓▓▓▓▓▓▓▓▓▓▓▓▓▓▓▓▓▓▓▓▓ ▓▓▓▓▓▓▓▓▓▓▓▓▓▓▓▓▓▓▓▓▓▓▓▓▓▓▓▓▓▓▓▓▓▓▓▓▓ ▓▓▓▓▓▓▓▓▓▓▓▓▓▓▓▓▓▓▓▓▓▓▓▓▓▓▓▓▓▓▓▓▓▓▓▓▓▓▓.

Protagonist: Blab bla blab bla bla bla blab.

Dylan: ▓▓▓▓▓▓▓▓▓▓▓▓▓▓▓▓▓▓▓▓▓▓▓▓▓▓▓▓.

Protagonist: Blab bla blab bla bla bla blab bla blab la blab bla blab bla blab bla bla bla blab bla blab la blab bla bla blab bla bla bla blab bla blab la blab bla bla bla blab bla bla bla blab bla blab la blab bla blab bla.

Dylan: ▓▓▓▓▓▓▓▓▓▓▓▓▓▓▓▓▓▓▓▓▓▓▓▓▓▓▓▓▓▓▓▓▓▓▓▓▓▓▓ ▓▓▓▓▓▓▓▓▓▓▓▓▓▓▓▓▓▓▓▓▓▓▓▓▓▓▓▓▓▓▓▓▓▓▓▓▓ ▓▓▓▓▓▓▓▓▓▓▓▓▓▓▓▓▓▓▓▓▓▓▓▓▓▓▓▓▓▓▓▓▓▓▓▓▓▓▓ ▓▓▓▓▓▓.

Protagonist: Blab bla blab bla bla bla blab bla blab la blab bla blab bla blab bla bla bla blab bla blab la blab bla bla blab bla bla bla blab bla blab la blab bla bla bla blab bla bla bla blab bla blab la blab bla blab bla blab la blab bla blab bla blab bla bla bla blab bla blab la blab bla bla blab bla bla bla blab bla blab la blab bla bla bla blab bla bla bla blab bla blab la blab bla blab bla.

Dylan: ████████████████████████████████████
██
██
██
██
██.

Protagonist: Blab bla blab bla bla bla blab bla blab la blab bla
blab bla blab bla bla bla blab bla blab la blab bla bla blab bla bla
bla blab bla blab la blab bla bla bla blab bla bla bla blab bla blab
la blab bla blab bla.

Dylan: ████████████████████████████████████
██
██████████.

Protagonist: Blab bla blab bla bla bla blab bla blab la blab bla
blab bla blab bla bla bla blab bla blab la blab bla bla blab bla bla
bla blab bla blab la blab bla bla bla blab bla bla bla blab bla blab
la blab bla blab bla blab bla blab la blab bla blab bla blab bla bla
bla blab bla blab la blab bla bla blab bla bla bla blab bla blab la
blab bla bla bla blab bla bla bla blab bla blab la blab bla blab bla.

Dylan: ████████████████████████████████████
██
██
██
██
██.

Protagonist: Blab bla blab bla bla bla blab bla blab la blab bla
blab bla blab bla bla bla blab bla blab la blab bla bla blab bla bla

bla blab bla blab la blab bla bla bla blab bla bla bla blab bla blab la blab bla blab bla.

Dylan: ████████████████████████████████████
████████████████████████████████
██
███████████.

Protagonist: Blab bla blab bla bla bla blab bla blab la blab bla blab bla blab bla bla bla blab bla blab la blab bla bla blab bla bla bla blab bla blab la blab bla bla bla blab bla bla bla blab bla blab la blab bla blab bla blab la blab bla blab bla blab bla bla bla blab bla blab la blab bla bla.

Dylan: ██
███████████████████████████████████
██
██████████████████████████████████
███████████████████████████.

Protagonist: Blab bla blab bla bla bla blab bla blab la blab bla blab bla blab bla bla bla blab bla blab la blab bla bla blab bla bla bla blab bla blab la blab bla bla bla blab bla bla bla blab bla blab la blab bla blab bla bla bla blab bla blab la blab bla blab bla blab bla bla bla blab bla blab la blab bla bla blab bla bla bla blab bla blab la blab bla bblab bla blab bla bla bla blab bla blab blab bla.

Dylan: ██
███████████████████████████████████
████████████████████████████████████
█████████████████████████████████
██████████████████████████████████
██████████████████████████████████████.

Protagonist: Blab bla blab bla bla bla blab bla blab la blab bla blab bla blab bla bla bla blab bla blab la blab bla bla blab bla bla bla.

Dylan: ▓▓
▓▓▓▓▓▓▓▓▓▓▓▓▓▓▓▓▓▓▓▓▓▓▓▓▓▓▓▓▓▓▓▓▓▓▓▓▓▓.

Protagonist: Blab bla blab bla bla bla blab bla blab la blab bla blab bla blab bla bla bla blab bla blab la blab bla bla blab bla bla bla blab bla blab la blab bla bla bla blab bla bla bla blab bla bla bla blab bla.

Dylan: ▓▓
▓▓▓▓▓▓▓▓▓▓▓▓▓▓▓▓▓▓▓▓▓▓▓▓▓▓▓▓▓▓▓▓▓▓▓▓▓▓
▓▓▓▓▓▓▓▓▓▓▓▓▓▓▓▓▓▓▓▓▓▓▓▓▓▓▓▓▓▓▓▓▓▓▓▓▓▓.

Protagonist: Blab bla blab bla bla bla blab bla blab la blab bla blab bla blab bla bla bla blab bla blab la blab bla bla blab bla bla bla blab bla blab la blab bla bla bla blab bla bla bla blab bla.

Dylan: ▓▓
▓▓▓▓▓▓▓▓▓▓▓▓▓▓▓▓▓▓▓▓▓▓▓▓▓▓▓▓▓▓▓▓▓▓▓▓▓▓
▓▓▓▓▓▓▓▓▓▓▓▓▓▓▓▓▓▓▓▓▓▓▓▓▓▓▓▓▓▓.

Protagonist: Blab bla blab bla bla bla blab bla blab la blab bla blab bla blab bla bla bla blab bla blab la blab bla bla blab bla bla bla blab bla blab la blab bla bla bla blab bla bla bla blab bla blab la blab bla blab bla.

Dylan: ▓▓
▓▓▓▓▓▓▓▓▓▓▓▓▓▓▓▓▓▓▓▓▓▓▓▓▓▓▓▓▓▓▓▓▓▓▓▓▓▓
▓▓▓▓▓▓▓▓▓▓▓▓▓▓▓▓▓▓▓▓▓▓▓▓▓▓▓▓▓▓▓▓▓▓▓▓▓▓
▓▓▓▓▓▓.

Protagonist: Blab bla blab bla bla bla blab bla blab la blab bla
blab bla blab bla bla bla blab bla blab la blab bla bla blab bla bla
bla blab bla blab la blab bla bla bla blab bla bla bla blab bla blab
la blab bla blab bla blab bla blab la blab bla blab bla blab bla bla
bla blab bla blab la blab bla bla blab bla bla bla blab bla blab la
blab bla bla bla blab bla bla bla blab bla blab la blab bla blab bla.

Dylan: ▬▬▬▬▬▬▬▬▬▬▬▬▬▬▬▬▬▬▬▬▬▬
▬▬▬▬▬▬▬▬▬▬▬▬▬▬▬▬▬▬▬▬▬▬
▬▬▬▬▬▬▬▬▬▬▬▬▬▬▬▬▬▬▬▬▬▬
▬▬▬▬▬▬▬▬▬▬▬▬▬▬▬▬▬▬▬
▬▬▬▬▬▬▬▬▬▬▬▬▬▬▬▬▬▬▬▬▬
▬▬▬▬▬▬▬▬.

Protagonist: Blab bla blab bla bla bla blab bla blab la blab bla
blab bla blab bla bla bla blab bla blab la blab bla bla blab bla bla
bla blab bla blab la blab bla bla bla blab bla bla bla blab bla blab
la blab bla blab bla.

Dylan: ▬▬▬▬▬▬▬▬▬▬▬▬▬▬▬▬▬▬▬▬▬▬
▬▬▬▬▬▬▬▬▬▬▬▬▬▬▬▬▬▬▬▬▬
▬▬▬▬▬▬▬▬▬▬▬▬▬▬▬▬▬▬▬▬▬▬
▬▬▬▬.

Protagonist: Blab bla blab bla bla bla blab bla blab la blab bla
blab bla blab bla bla bla blab bla blab la blab bla bla blab bla bla
bla blab bla blab la blab bla bla bla blab bla bla bla blab bla blab
la blab bla blab bla blab bla blab la blab bla blab bla blab bla bla
bla blab bla blab la blab bla bla blab bla bla bla blab bla blab la
blab bla bla bla blab bla bla bla blab bla blab la blab bla blab bla.

Dylan: ▬▬▬▬▬▬▬▬▬▬▬▬▬▬▬▬▬▬▬▬▬▬
▬▬▬▬▬▬▬▬▬▬▬▬▬▬▬▬▬▬▬▬▬
▬▬▬▬▬▬▬▬▬▬▬▬▬▬▬▬▬▬▬▬▬▬

[redacted].

Protagonist: Blab bla blab bla bla bla blab bla blab la blab bla blab bla blab bla bla bla blab bla blab la blab bla bla blab bla bla bla blab bla blab la blab bla bla bla blab bla bla bla blab bla blab la blab bla blab bla.

Dylan: [redacted].

Protagonist: Blab bla blab bla bla bla blab bla blab la blab bla blab bla blab bla bla bla blab bla blab la blab bla bla blab bla bla bla blab bla blab la blab bla bla bla blab bla bla bla blab bla blab la blab bla blab bla blab la blab bla blab bla blab bla bla bla blab bla blab la blab bla bla.

And here is the identical conversation passage in reverse, so it shows what I am hearing, which is my own voice only. Between you and me, by the time this conversation took place I was getting a little tired of the subject myself – so I am droning on, and what I am saying is not that interesting, and much can be found elsewhere in this book anyway:

Protagonist: [redacted].

Dylan: Blab bla blab bla bla bla blab bla blab la blab bla blab bla

blab bla bla bla blab bla blab la blab bla bla blab bla bla bla blab bla blab la blab bla bla bla blab bla bla bla blab bla blab la blab bla blab bla blab bla bla bla blab bla blab.

Protagonist: ████████████████████████████████
████████████████████████████████
████████████████████████████████████
████████████████████████████████
████████████████████████████████████
██████████████████████████.

Dylan: Blab bla blab bla bla bla blab bla blab la blab bla blab bla blab bla bla bla blab bla blab la blab bla bla blab bla bla bla blab bla blab la blab bla bla bla blab bla bla bla blab bla blab la blab bla blab bla blab bla bla bla blab bla blab la blab bla blab bla blab bla bla bla blab bla blab la blab bla bla blab bla bla bla blab bla blab la blab.

Protagonist: ████████████████████████████████
████████████████████████████████
████████████████████████████████████
████████████████████████████████
██████████████████████████.

Dylan: Blab bla blab bla bla bla blab bla blab la blab bla blab bla blab bla bla bla blab bla blab la blab bla bla blab bla bla bla blab bla blab la blab bla bla bla blab bla bla bla blab bla blab la blab bla blab bla blab bla bla bla blab bla blab la blab bla blab bla blab bla bla bla blab.

Protagonist: ████████████████████████████████
████████████████████████████████
████████████████████████████████████
████████████████████████████████████

███████████████████████████████████████
████████████.

Dylan: Blab bla blab bla bla bla blab bla blab la blab bla blab bla
blab bla bla bla blab bla blab la blab bla bla blab bla bla bla blab
bla blab la blab bla bla bla blab bla bla bla blab bla blab la blab
bla blab bla blab bla bla bla blab bla blab la blab bla blab bla
blab bla bla bla blab bla bla blab bla blab la blab bla blab bla bla.

Protagonist: ████████████████████████████████████
██████████████████████████████████
██
████████████████████████████████████
██
██████████████████████.

Dylan: Blab bla blab bla bla bla blab bla blab la blab bla blab bla
blab bla bla bla blab bla blab la blab bla bla blab bla bla bla blab
bla blab la blab bla bla bla blab bla bla bla blab bla blab la blab
bla blab bla blab bla bla bla blab bla blab la blab bla blab bla
blab bla bla bla blab bla blab bla bla bla blab bla blab bla bla bla
blab bla blab bla bla bla blab.

Protagonist: ████████████████████████████████████
██████████████████████████████████
██
████████████████████████████████████
███████████████████████████████████████.

Dylan: Blab bla blab bla bla bla blab bla blab la blab bla blab bla
blab bla bla bla blab bla blab la blab bla bla blab bla bla bla blab
bla blab la blab bla bla bla blab bla bla bla blab bla blab la blab
bla blab bla blab bla bla bla blab bla blab la blab bla blab bla
blab bla bla bla blab bla blab bla bla bla blab bla bla bla.

Protagonist: ██
███████████████████████████████████████
██
██████████████████████████████████████
██
████████████.

Dylan: Blab bla blab bla bla bla blab bla blab la blab bla blab bla
blab bla bla bla blab bla blab la blab bla bla blab bla bla bla blab
bla blab la blab bla bla bla blab bla bla bla blab bla blab la blab
bla blab bla blab bla bla bla blab bla blab la blab bla blab bla
blab bla bla bla blab bla blab bla bla bla.

Protagonist: ██
███████████████████████████████████████
███
██████████████████████████████████████
██
██
████████████████████████.

Dylan: Blab bla blab bla bla bla blab bla blab la blab bla blab bla
blab bla bla bla blab bla blab la blab bla bla blab bla bla bla blab
bla blab la blab bla bla bla blab bla bla bla blab bla blab la blab
bla blab bla blab bla bla bla blab bla blab la blab bla blab bla
blab bla bla bla blab bla blab la blab bla bla blab bla bla bla blab
bla blab la blab bla bblab bla blab bla bla bla blab bla blab la
blab bla.

Protagonist: ██
███████████████████████████████████████
██
███████████████████████████████████.

Dylan: Blab bla blab bla bla bla blab bla blab la blab bla blab bla blab bla bla bla blab bla blab la blab bla bla blab bla bla bla blab bla blab la blab bla bla bla blab bla bla bla blab bla blab la blab bla blab bla blab bla bla bla blab bla blab la blab bla blab bla blab bla bla bla blab.

Protagonist: █████████████████████████████████████
████████████████████████████████████
██
█████████████████████████████████████
██
██
███████████████.

Dylan: Blab bla blab bla bla bla blab bla blab la blab bla blab bla blab bla bla bla blab bla blab la blab bla bla blab bla bla bla blab bla blab la blab bla bla bla blab bla bla bla blab bla blab la blab bla blab bla bla bla blab bla blab la blab bla blab bla blab bla bla bla blab bla blab la blab bla bla blab bla bla bla blab bla blab la blab bla bblab bla blab bla bla bla blab bla blab la blab bla.

Protagonist: ██████████████████████████████████
███████████████████████████████████████
██████.

Dylan: Blab bla blab bla bla bla blab bla blab la blab bla blab bla blab bla bla bla blab bla blab la blab bla bla blab bla bla bla.

Protagonist: ██████████████████████████████████
███████████████████████████████████
█████████████████████████████████.

Dylan: Blab bla blab bla bla bla blab bla blab la blab bla blab bla

blab bla bla bla blab bla blab la blab bla bla blab bla bla bla blab bla blab la blab bla bla bla blab bla bla bla blab bla.

Protagonist: ▓▓▓▓▓▓▓▓▓▓▓▓▓▓▓▓▓▓▓▓.

Dylan: Blab bla blab bla bla bla blab.

Protagonist: ▓▓▓▓▓▓▓▓▓▓▓▓▓▓▓▓▓▓▓▓▓
▓▓▓▓▓▓▓▓▓▓▓▓▓▓▓▓▓▓▓▓▓▓
▓▓▓▓▓▓▓▓▓▓▓▓▓▓▓▓▓▓▓▓▓▓
▓▓▓▓▓▓▓▓▓▓▓.

Dylan: Blab bla blab bla bla bla blab bla blab la blab bla blab bla blab bla bla bla blab bla blab la blab bla bla blab bla bla bla blab bla blab la blab bla bla bla blab bla bla bla blab bla blab la blab bla blab bla.

Protagonist: ▓▓▓▓▓▓▓▓▓▓▓▓▓▓▓▓▓▓▓▓▓
▓▓▓▓▓▓▓▓▓▓▓▓▓▓▓▓▓▓▓▓▓▓
▓▓▓▓▓▓▓▓▓▓▓▓▓▓▓▓▓▓▓▓▓▓
▓▓▓▓▓▓▓▓▓▓▓▓▓▓▓▓▓▓▓▓▓▓
▓▓▓▓▓▓▓▓▓▓▓▓▓▓▓▓▓▓▓▓▓▓
▓▓▓▓▓.

Dylan: Blab bla blab bla bla bla blab bla blab la blab bla blab bla blab bla bla bla blab bla blab la blab bla bla blab bla bla bla blab bla blab la blab bla bla bla blab bla bla bla blab bla blab la blab bla blab bla blab bla blab la blab bla blab bla blab bla bla bla blab bla blab la blab bla bla blab bla bla bla blab bla blab la blab bla bla bla blab bla bla bla blab la blab bla blab bla.

Protagonist: ▓▓▓▓▓▓▓▓▓▓▓▓▓▓▓▓▓▓▓▓▓
▓▓▓▓▓▓▓▓▓▓▓▓▓▓▓▓▓▓▓▓▓▓

██
██████████████████████.

Dylan: Blab bla blab bla bla bla blab bla blab la blab bla blab bla
blab bla bla bla blab bla blab la blab bla bla blab bla bla bla blab
bla blab la blab bla bla bla blab bla bla bla blab bla blab la blab
bla blab bla.

Protagonist: ████████████████████████████████
██
██
██
██
██.

Dylan: Blab bla blab bla bla bla blab bla blab la blab bla blab bla
blab bla bla bla blab bla blab la blab bla bla blab bla bla bla blab
bla blab la blab bla bla bla blab bla bla bla blab bla blab la blab
bla blab bla blab bla blab la blab bla blab bla blab bla bla bla
blab bla blab la blab bla bla blab bla bla bla blab bla blab la blab
bla bla bla blab bla bla blab bla blab la blab bla blab bla.

Protagonist: ████████████████████████████████
██
██
██████████████████████.

Dylan: Blab bla blab bla bla bla blab bla blab la blab bla blab bla
blab bla bla bla blab bla blab la blab bla bla blab bla bla bla blab
bla blab la blab bla bla bla blab bla bla bla blab bla blab la blab
bla blab bla.

Protagonist: ████████████████████████████████
██

.

Dylan: Blab bla blab bla bla bla blab bla blab la blab bla blab bla blab bla bla bla blab bla blab la blab bla bla blab bla bla bla blab bla blab la blab bla bla bla blab bla bla bla blab bla blab la blab bla blab bla blab bla blab la blab bla blab bla blab bla bla bla blab bla.

Protagonist:

.

Dylan: Blab bla blab bla bla bla blab bla blab la blab bla blab bla blab bla bla bla blab bla blab la blab bla bla blab bla bla bla blab bla blab la blab bla bla bla blab bla bla bla blab bla blab la blab bla blab bla blab bla bla bla blab bla blab la blab bla bla bla blab bla bla bla blab bla bla bla blab bla blab la blab bla bblab bla blab bla bla bla blab bla blab la blab bla.

Protagonist:

.

Dylan: Blab bla blab bla bla bla blab bla blab la blab bla blab bla blab bla bla bla blab bla blab la blab bla bla blab bla bla bla blab bla bla blab bla bla bla bla blab bla blab la blab bla bla blab bla.

Protagonist: ████████████████████████████████████
████████████████████████████████████
██.

Dylan: Blab bla blab bla bla bla blab bla blab la blab bla blab bla blab bla bla bla blab bla blab la blab bla bla blab bla bla bla blab bla blab la blab bla bla bla blab bla bla bla blab bla.

Protagonist: ████████████████████████████████████
████████████████████████████████████
██.

Dylan: Blab bla blab bla bla bla blab bla blab la blab bla blab bla blab bla bla bla blab bla blab la blab bla bla blab bla bla bla blab bla blab la blab bla bla bla blab bla bla bla blab bla.

Protagonist: ████████████████████████████████████
████████████████████████████████████
████████████████████████████████████
██████████████.

Dylan: Blab bla blab bla bla bla blab bla blab la blab bla blab bla blab bla bla bla blab bla blab la blab bla bla blab bla bla bla blab bla blab la blab bla bla bla blab bla bla bla blab bla blab la blab bla blab bla.

Protagonist: ████████████████████████████████████
████████████████████████████████████
████████████████████████████████████
████████████████████████████████████
████████████████████████████████████.

Dylan: Blab bla blab bla bla bla blab bla blab la blab bla blab bla

blab bla bla bla blab bla blab la blab bla bla blab bla bla bla blab
bla blab la blab bla bla bla blab bla bla bla blab bla blab la blab
bla blab bla blab bla blab la blab bla blab bla blab bla bla bla
blab bla blab la blab bla bla blab bla bla bla blab bla blab la blab
bla bla bla blab bla bla bla blab bla blab la blab bla blab bla.

Protagonist: ███████████████████████████████████
████████████████████████████████
██
███████████████████.

Dylan: Blab bla blab bla bla bla blab bla blab la blab bla blab bla
blab bla bla bla blab bla blab la blab bla bla blab bla bla bla blab
bla blab la blab bla bla bla blab bla bla bla blab bla blab la blab
bla blab bla.

Protagonist: ███████████████████████████████████
██████████████████████████████████
███████████████████████████████████████
██████████████████████████████████████
██████████████████████████████████████
██████████████████████████████████.

Dylan: Blab bla blab bla bla bla blab bla blab la blab bla blab bla
blab bla bla bla blab bla blab la blab bla bla blab bla bla bla blab
bla blab la blab bla bla bla blab bla bla bla blab bla blab la blab
bla blab bla blab bla blab la blab bla blab bla blab bla bla bla
blab bla blab la blab bla bla blab bla bla bla blab bla blab la blab
bla bla bla blab bla bla bla blab bla blab la blab bla blab bla.

Protagonist: ███████████████████████████████████
█████████████████████████████████████
██
███████████████████.

60

Dylan: Blab bla blab bla bla bla blab bla blab la blab bla blab bla blab bla bla bla blab bla blab la blab bla bla blab bla bla bla blab bla blab la blab bla bla bla blab bla bla bla blab bla blab la blab bla blab bla.

Protagonist: ▉▉▉▉▉▉▉▉▉▉▉▉▉▉▉▉▉▉▉▉▉▉▉▉▉▉
▉▉▉▉▉▉▉▉▉▉▉▉▉▉▉▉▉▉▉▉▉▉▉▉▉▉
▉▉▉▉▉▉▉▉▉▉▉▉▉▉▉▉▉▉▉▉▉▉▉▉▉▉▉
▉▉▉▉▉▉▉▉.

As you can see, it's not much of a conversation. After forty-five minutes I pretend I am feeling unwell, and Dylan is gracious enough to leave.

I just had an amusing afterthought: as Dylan was not listening to what I was saying I might have just said bla-bla-bla anyway all the way through whenever it was my turn to talk. He would not have noticed. I believe in the intelligence of my reader and think that I can probably spare you an eight-page illustration of this from my perspective (what I am hearing), still here is a short sample illustration for the less fortunate:

Protagonist: Blab bla blab bla bla bla blab bla blab la blab bla blab bla blab bla bla bla blab bla blab la blab bla bla blab bla bla bla blab bla blab la blab bla bla bla blab bla bla bla blab bla blab la blab bla blab bla blab bla bla bla blab bla blab la blab bla blab bla blab bla bla bla blab bla blab bla bla bla blab bla blab bla bla bla blab.

Dylan: Blab bla blab bla bla bla blab bla blab la blab bla blab bla blab bla bla bla blab bla blab la blab bla bla blab bla bla bla blab bla blab la blab bla bla bla blab bla bla bla blab bla blab la blab bla blab bla blab bla bla bla blab bla blab la blab bla blab bla blab bla bla bla blab bla blab bla bla bla blab.

Protagonist: Blab bla blab bla bla bla blab bla blab la blab bla blab bla blab bla bla bla blab bla blab la blab bla bla blab bla bla bla blab bla blab la blab bla bla bla blab bla bla bla blab bla blab bla blab la blab bla blab bla blab bla bla bla blab bla blab la blab bla blab bla blab bla bla bla.

Dylan: Blab bla blab bla bla bla blab bla blab la blab bla blab bla blab bla bla bla blab bla blab la blab bla bla blab bla bla bla blab bla blab la blab bla bla bla blab bla bla bla blab bla blab la blab bla blab bla blab bla bla bla blab bla blab la blab bla blab bla blab bla bla bla.

Protagonist: Blab bla blab bla bla bla blab bla blab la blab bla blab bla blab bla bla bla blab bla blab la blab bla bla blab bla bla bla blab bla blab la blab bla bla bla blab bla bla bla blab bla bla bla bla bla bla bla blab bla blab la blab bla bla bla blab bla bla bla blab bla bla blab bla bla blab bla bla bla.

Dylan: Blab bla blab bla bla bla blab bla blab la blab bla blab bla blab bla bla bla blab bla blab la blab bla bla blab bla bla bla blab bla blab la blab bla bla bla blab bla bla bla blab bla blab la blab bla bla blabla blab bla blab la blab bla bla bla blab bla bla bla blab bla bla blab bla bla blab bla bla bla.

I think if you don't get the point of this by now you probably shouldn't be reading this book anyway.

Unfortunately, Legal has made a hash of the whole thing by insisting that all medical stuff be redacted. I think that is probably right as far as Dylan's side of the conversation is concerned. He is a private and shy guy, and I cannot see him agreeing to have his medical record splashed out in all its gory detail in the midst of a comic novel about cancer. As for my part of the conversation, I would have happily signed a disclaimer, as I am a bit of an exhibitionist and love talking about my cancer. And this is where the office revolt began: Legal and Editorial ganged up against the proprietor.

[Proprietor's note: I know from long experience that whilst I can overrule almost anything Editorial by sheer brute force, my hands are bound by Legal. Legal always wins. This is just one of those things. Well, on this occasion Legal and Editorial got together and really screwed their proprietor: I had a row about nothing with somebody in Legal a few weeks ago, and I still sense the resentment every time I walk into their department. I know that Editorial is really worried about the endless repetition of medical stuff, which they find really unappetizing and boring. I am still baffled by this. I mean they don't get it, do they? This is at the core a book about a personal battle with cancer, not some light entertainment. They sprang a trap on me: Editorial got what it wanted, and Legal its revenge.]

Since the operation my sleeping pattern has changed: I fall asleep very late and wake up very early, usually by about 5. When I cannot sleep I like to invent characters that are somehow related to the particular place or situation I am in. I am charmed by Claridge's history, and I thought it would be amusing to introduce another character into the narrative, in case you are getting bored with me. So let me introduce you to The Political Prisoner: Many years ago he was on the run from the French Secret Service, for reasons long forgotten, and his goal was to seek asylum in the Ecuadorian Embassy, but in his panic he took a wrong turn at Hyde Park Corner, a mistake easily made when you are in a foreign city with a bunch of aggressive gun-toting Frogs on your heels. His knowledge of London landmarks was rudimentary, and he mistook Claridge's for the embassy building. A major international political crisis ensued, expertly hushed up by all countries involved and never publicly reported. The Political Prisoner is a bit hazy about dates – this is what decades at Claridge's will do to you – but he is pretty sure that Margaret Thatcher was Prime Minister at the time. I completely understand. I too am getting a bit vague about outside facts after only a week, so imagine what happens to your brain after three decades in here! I first thought that somebody at the Foreign Office clearly had a sense of historical continuity or a dry sense humour, because as part of the ensuing diplomatic solution the British Government ceded Room 212 to Ecuador and The Political Prisoner moved in. He has been there ever since, miserably but very comfortably. The decision actually had nothing do with humour or a sense of history. Margaret Thatcher was merely following the example of Winston Churchill. Room 212 was where the exiled king and the pregnant queen of Yugoslavia lived during the Second World War. Their son, in order to preserve his right to the throne, needed to be born on Yugoslavian soil. To this end Churchill devised the idea of ceding 212 to Yugoslavia for the day of the prince's birth, imagine Whitehall mandarins preparing the paperwork! It was one of those wonderful poetic gestures Churchill was capable of – elegant, sentimental – and it turned out useless because the little prince never became king. Margaret Thatcher merely copied the format without achieving any of the poetry.

The Political Prisoner is without romance – an unhappy, angry man, stuck in his room. Even the Ecuadorians sometimes forget about him, and the unpaid bills for room and extras cause Claridge's management considerable anxiety. Yet in the end everything is always settled, although late. Nobody wants to make a fuss; nobody wants to cause another political crisis. Nobody in international politics has the will or patience to solve the matter and free The Political Prisoner. It would be too much work: parliamentary backbenchers the world over could cause a fuss and ask officials uncomfortable questions. Resolving the matter for good would be too exhausting and not worth the political capital expended, and in the end it is not necessary: Everybody knows that one day The Political Prisoner will die. His tin coffin will be removed surreptitiously in the middle of the night via the service entrance, and his room will be lavishly redecorated and rented out again, at a premium, to Yugoslavians who feel sentimental about their country's royal past. Time is not of the essence.

The visitor traffic has been prodigious, and I would not be surprised if carpet replacement turns up on my final bill, the same way Britney's jacuzzi turned up on hers. Would she have noticed? I wonder. As she was on tour was it tax-deductible? I can just imagine a huge fight between her tax attorney and US revenue, generating tens of thousands of dollars in extra legal fees. Anyway, I just realised, I need not worry about my final bill; Ivor will take care of it, carpet or not. Like Britney he won't even notice.

Now that The Bitch has moved in full time I am feeling much happier. I know that dogs are definitely permitted at Claridge's, but I am telling the front desk anyway, so that they know, in case she needs to be accounted for in a fire drill or something.

Returning from our morning walk in Green Park and coming into the lobby I realise that I am jealous of The Bitch. Living at Claridge's requires a certain attitude, best expressed when crossing the lobby, a nonchalance that shows, to yourself mainly, that you are not awed by the place. In two days here The Bitch has developed her she-does-not-give-a-fuck saunter to absolute perfection. By comparison I am still a beginner, and my lobby-crossing remains a little tentative and hit-and-miss. The Bitch has no such problem. How does she do it?

Andrea comes for lunch. I have been in love with her for decades, and we always flirt outrageously. She is smart, funny and sassy. We are having a grand old time, discussing what she might do after her retirement from the British Council. What will they do without her? Anyway, I don't think she will be sitting at home bored and doing embroidery. She will be very busy with a lot of fun things. I suggest that maybe she would like to do a book with Ridinghouse? I would love to have her on our list of authors. One of the subjects we discuss is the rather unappetizing opportunism of certain lawyers, a form of legal ambulance chasing.

At 2.30 sharp Penny arrives. I am in love with her too, and the two women are clearly a bit put out at finding each other in my suite at the same time. I am beginning to feel like Truman Capote in the company of his swans. He was a complete idiot to betray their confidence. What was he thinking? I would never do such a thing.

Andrea, by the way, brought as a gift a book about hot-air ballooning. Why? Is it a coded message?

[Excerpt from email to Andrea]
'Darling – I loved our lunch. Can we please repeat it before I move out. I know you find North London a bit far out and never visit. Regarding our conversation about ███████████, ████████████████████ and I were gossiping about him only yesterday, and I said that he reminded me a bit of a hyena, you know like one in an Attenborough nature programme, the setting grassland, the odd tree, the landscape shimmering with heat, a buffalo (?) bellowing in the distance, flies buzzing, Attenborough's soothing voice-over (I think you get the picture). The lions have killed a zebra, and we are halfway through the meal. The lions are bloated with zebra, smeared with blood, and there is the sound of crunching bones in the air (imagine the stench!), and the hyenas are hanging about nervously on the fringe, impatiently yacking away, trying to get closer without

endangering their lives, trying to get a scrap, any scrap, and they usually get something, usually something disgusting like a bit of entrail or a zebra's ear. It's a hard way to make a living, and it is exceedingly dangerous. In case you are really interested there is a clip on YouTube of a lion killing a hyena (http://www.youtube.com/watch?v= 7l90lM0-9Yg): it looks like the lion is really enjoying it, payback time for scores of hyenas having marginally pissed him off over years, but all added up here and discharged at one poor hyena who can't quite understand where all that anger is suddenly coming from. It nearly makes you feel sorry for hyenas. – If you can't do lunch or dinner there is always tea here, every day from 3 to 6.*

[Excerpt from The Diary of The Political Prisoner, Room 212] 'Have started searching room for safe place to hide my diary so that THEY won't find it. If I hold on to it one day it will be published and might win me accolades and a prize, like POLITICAL PRISONER OF THE YEAR or something. I am longing to get out of here and re-join polite society. It's been too long.'

* [Editorial note: It is not quite clear what the author is getting at here, but we included the passage anyway, it demonstrates a certain poetic aptitude that is so soundly missing elsewhere in this book.]

4

In the afternoon I do the Mayfair gallery rounds, there is a so-so Sigmar Polke and Gerhard Richter exhibition at Christie's new gallery on New Bond Street. 'Curated' is too big a word for the show. It looks more like an intern has spent an afternoon calling around for loans. There is also the Impressionist and Modern preview at Sotheby's, and of course the annual Dale Chihuly exhibition at Halcyon Gallery. Halcyon is big, brash and very expensive and conveniently dead opposite Sotheby's, and I look at Dale's exhibitions there every summer (they seem to be on every summer, at least). The gallery is packed with spiky glass objects and tons of people in hushed silence, as if they are looking at something truly wonderful. I only go in because I can never quite believe how pointless and ugly the stuff is. The fact that anyone actually buys these monstrosities voluntarily just blows my mind. The idea that you would go in there, pick one of these things, actually make a choice, sign a huge cheque and have the object in question carefully packed and shipped and installed in your home or wherever you are planning to put it, is hard to believe. I mean there is more craft and sense of proportion in the display at the tackiest Murano glassblower's in Venice. The stuff here is just big, big, and then even bigger. You can barely get past it at Halcyon without the danger of impaling yourself. There are endless chandeliers, some dangling right down to the floor, and some sort of barge so overloaded with glass that the whole thing looks as if it might capsize any moment and noisily implode. There are also smaller wall objects and the odd 'vase' or oversized 'ashtray' or whatever you want to call them. If you linger too long in front of one of the objects a sharply dressed girl with a pricelist will spot you and come over for a 'chat'. The trick is to look like you are just streaking through. Pretending that you are busy on your mobile phone works too. Anyway, I am safe: with the scar and the snot-blown front I am beyond consideration. I am lucky actually that security is not instructed to escort me off the premises.

Dale's work is now everywhere, from the Museum of Fine Arts in Boston (where they really should know better) down to Harrods. The store commissioned a huge chandelier for one of their staircases only a few months ago. No surprise there; taste was never a problem at Harrods. Chihuly chandeliers these days go up in upmarket lobbies the world over, like some nasty fungal infection except this one is ominously growing in glass.

One day, I comfort myself, all of this will come to an abrupt end, and this is how: one of these hideous, multi-ton objects will lose its moorings because material fatigue has set in or some steel cable has oxidised or whatever, and it will come crashing down, just like that. I can't say where in the world this will happen, it could be at the museum in Boston or the escalator hall at Harrods or in some luxury condominium lobby in Miami, it doesn't matter. It will happen somewhere. Hopefully it will happen in the middle of the night when nobody is about, so nobody will get injured or, God forbid, killed. The next morning health and safety teams all over the globe will swing into action and, without much ado, take down every single Chihuly chandelier they can get their hands on. The chandelier in the foyer at Claridge's will be de-installed before the first guests arrive for breakfast. Most of them won't even notice that it has gone. Private owners will follow suit. Inevitably somebody will make a movie of the whole episode, inevitably called *The Chihuly Incident*. It will be a bit like

Independence Day, you know the one about the hundreds of gigantic communicating spaceships ready to take over Earth, with some annoying geek busy stopping it from happening. Now I have tried watching *Independence Day* at least three times paying extra attention to the technical details, but I have never managed to figure out how it supposedly works or why this should be in any way interesting. I have never made it to the end because every time I've gotten so bored and have turned the DVD off in mid-film. *The Chihuly Incident* will be much easier to understand – one Health and Safety alert globally and it is all over. It will be difficult to pad this out to ninety minutes, but thankfully that is not my problem.

Returning from the flower shop we cross the lobby, and I watch The Bitch carefully out of the corner of my eye, and she does it again. If this was an Olympic sport she would get a score-board-shattering flush of tens every time. But then I realise that there is something wrong here. She is not really trying. It's second nature for her. It's in the genes, and she could not do it any other way even if she tried. It's part of what makes the breed so charming, that little scruffy-looking beast with this disproportionate attitude. It might even be part of the Kennel Club border terrier breeding standard. I am sure it is, it makes a lot of sense. I can stop feeling jealous: she isn't really trying; it's just her default setting on everything. I can relax. Scoring a border terrier's not-giving-a-fuck saunter is as pointless as giving medals to giraffes for their long necks.

The following afternoon I pay a visit to the new Kallos Gallery on Davies Street. It is the brainchild of Lorne Thyssen-Bornemisza, the son of Heini, the billionaire industrialist whose collection is today housed in its own museum in Madrid. Lorne has carved out his own niche and collects choice Greek antiquities. Now he has gone commercial, and his gallery had opened a few weeks before with great fanfare, a huge reception on the premises followed by a party at Claridge's for several hundred guests, with one of the exhibits, a seated archaic Greek goddess blown up to about two metres and recreated in ice as a centrepiece in the hotel's ballroom. I know about all this from the newspapers but also from my friend Robin, who went to the party and would not shut up about it. People can be such glamour whores. Everybody, apparently, was there, including the Prince of Wales but also, strangely, Colin Renfrew, Cambridge professor and famous crusader against archaeological looting and private ownership of antiquities. I would love to ask him what he was doing there. Undercover research?

I get to the gallery and ring the doorbell. A glamorous blonde looks up from her computer and spots me through the window. She comes up to the entrance and blocks it awkwardly with her body so that the door opens only two inches or so:

'YES?!?'

'Uh, I would like to look at your exhibition please.'

'Well, you have to be quick, we close in five minutes.'

She reluctantly lets me in. Now I know that I am not looking my best, glassy-eyed from the painkillers, and there is of course the scar, gory and angry-looking, and the unfortunate bloody-snot shirt-front. My haircut is overdue too, and I have not had a shave for weeks. Still, has somebody not told her that today you can no longer judge by appearances?

She returns to her computer, and I take a good look around. There are only about fifteen objects on display, every single one absolutely exquisite. My favourite is a tiny sixth-century BC bronze horse, about three inches tall. It miraculously manages to be highly stylised and appear naturalistic at the same time. Magic, pure magic. As I am looking a young man addresses me: 'Good afternoon, sir. May I introduce myself, my name is Glenn, I am the managing director of Kallos Gallery.'

He did not judge me by the scar or the shuffle or the shirt-front; he just saw me looking at things and drew his own conclusion. You can always tell when somebody is really looking. I tell him my name. A conversation ensues. We talk about the works on display, his ambition for the gallery, the success of the opening. Was I collecting myself, what about my areas of interest? I tell him a bit, tell him about my own business, talk about Ridinghouse. He is intelligent and engaging. By now he has clocked the scar. He looks at it, looks away, looks again, looks away again, but he is too polite to pop the question, so I help him out and explain.

'I am so very sorry, sir.'
'Oh, don't worry, the operation went really well, and the doctors are very happy with the outcome. I am recuperating at Claridge's, so there is really nothing to complain about.'
He lightens up.
'Do you enjoy being at Claridge's?'
'Yes, of course. What is there not to enjoy?'
'My boss always stays there when he is in London. He rents the royal suite. It's the biggest in the hotel, and the most expensive. It comes with two full-time butlers.'
'Really?'
'Yes.'
'Amazing.'
I am genuinely taken aback; I mean what can you possibly do with two butlers?
'How do you find the staff?' he continues.
'They are all absolutely wonderful, quite exceptional.'
'That's interesting. My boss says that you should be strict with them to begin with and then you get excellent service.'
'Well, that is not my experience. I charmed everybody's pants off from arrival and tip very generously and now the entire hotel seems to revolve around me and my dog. It's wonderful.'
I tell him about The Bitch.

'Oh she sounds great, bring her in the next time you come past,' the blonde chips in.

'I will, thank you.'

What a very odd idea, to treat staff harshly so that you finally get good service. It does not make any sense, and my hunch is that all this has more to do with Lorne's complicated relationship with his notoriously difficult late father than any true insight into how to treat or not to treat servants, but I keep this thought to myself. By now everybody working at the gallery is taking part in our conversation. The frosty blonde turns out not frosty at all but charming and bright and funny. We all are having a very good time. He takes me to the basement where there are a few more objects on display. The most astonishing is a silver dish with a small, minutely detailed, three-dimensional Medusa's head at the centre. It is obviously a cult object, and you can imagine the Medusa's head slowly surfacing as the liquid, blood or wine, is drained away. It is an object beautiful and scary at the same time. It's chilling.

I finally look at my watch and realise that I am running late: 'Oh dear, I must go back to the hotel, I have guests arriving soon. Well, it was a real pleasure meeting you all.'

We say good-bye and I promise to come back soon and have another look at their exhibits. I promise that I will bring The Bitch. The blonde is truly delightful.

Walking back to the hotel I am still thinking about the little horse and the Medusa bowl but also about the two butlers. What could you possibly do with them? I mean two of them, 24/7? Just thinking about them is exhausting! What, I wonder, would Britney do? Of course, it's obvious, isn't it? She would have management install a racetrack in the sitting room of the Royal Suite, it sure is big enough. If I were her I would have the jacuzzi moved from the bathroom to the sitting room, right to the centre of the track. I am sure plumbing would be a nightmare, but I have full confidence in Claridge's technicians.

Britney could then sit in the jacuzzi and watch the two butlers race the track like a pair of sleek greyhounds. Yes, this is perfect. The tea party ends at six, my guests leave, and I take a nap.

A very bad dream: I am entertaining people for tea in my sitting room. As you can tell my mind no longer wanders very far. The party is in full swing, everybody is having a great time, the women are all dressed to the nines in ball gowns. Cate Blanchett is there, in what looks to me like an Oscar de la Renta bright orange taffeta red-carpet number and serious diamond jewellery, possibly Graff, but I am not completely sure. She is wonderful. I cannot remember what we all are talking about, it does not matter. Everybody is smiling and gracious, and we are all eating pizza. [Editor: Why pizza?] [Author: I don't know. It's a dream.] [Editor: Silly me.] And then gradually expressions change, everybody is staring at me in disbelief, disbelief turns into disgust, and disgust turns into horror. I am looking down my front and there is greasy tomato paste everywhere. How can I be so messy, I wonder. Everybody is looking at me, and the conversation has stopped. I suddenly realise that I am not covered in tomato paste but blood, lots of it. When I look down at my left shoulder there is a crater, pulsating with blood like a burbling spring. The women start screaming, and Cate rushes over and puts a napkin over the wound. There is absolute pandemonium, and I pass out.

I wake up with a start. I am freezing cold and in terrible pain, as if my body had taken the dream literally. I cannot believe how bad I am feeling. I order a club sandwich for dinner and drink some whisky. It takes me about two hours to warm up, regain my composure and calm down.

The following day at about six pm I take The Bitch for a long walk in Green Park. The Bitch spots in the distance one of those big, ugly dogs with pointed snout and slightly slitty eyes, muscle-bound as if designed solely to kill others of its species in the smoky backroom spaces that nobody has actually ever seen in reality where illegal dog fighting takes place. The dog looks like somebody had successfully crossed a pig with a pit bull, which is of course impossible, so it must have happened some other way. This one drags his owner energetically across the lawn. He turns out to be six months old. The Bitch runs over, I caution her that this may not be such a smart idea. She ignores me, and the two tumble about for a little. Sometimes I wonder about The Bitch's taste in men, but she would probably say the same about me, so I leave it and say nothing.

We return via Bond Street, which by this time has calmed down a bit. The pavement looks hot and exhausted from all that afternoon shopping.

5

I cross the hotel lobby to the concierge desk, I greet the guy on duty who is lovely, and we have a little chat. I am only a little impatient but do not show it. He engages me in a conversation about The Bitch and his brother's problem with his two border terrier puppies, aged 5 months, if I remember correctly, and how the two are tearing the brother's place apart. I am thinking about The Bitch at that age and how she and her friend Jezebel (same breed, same age; they are still best friends, in case you were wondering) and how it was impossible to keep their minds focused on anything, absolutely anything. The two would just fall into some reverie and joyously tear the crap out of each other. Now you can engage me in this sort of conversation any time you like, and it turns non-dog people into white paroxysms of rage to have two dog people do this because it excludes them from conversation, and it is in the end a tad rude. I completely understand. But at this point I am only half interested in it, because a) for me this is already the fourth conversation of the day I had with a staff member in the lobby on the subject of The Bitch, and whilst I love The Bitch dearly even I have a limit as to the number of conversations of this kind per day I can actually endure, and b) I want to go upstairs, have a shower and get ready for the arrival of my friends for dinner. So I gently turn the conversation on to the subject I am really interested in, away from the impossibility of teaching two border terrier puppies manners when they are only focused on each other and a good energetic romp. We all know, after all, that this is impossible.

'Uh, could you please check my 7.30 reservation at the hotel's restaurant for me, please?'

'Of course, sir.'

He energetically does the keyboard thing.

One burst, another burst and another. He is efficient. It is routine.

'When did you make the reservation?'

'Uh, last week.'

'Where?'

'With one of your colleagues at this desk, actually.'

The colleague had given me a huge spiel about how hard it was to get into the place (I know, eight months for 'normal people', who are those who are not staying here), had booked the table by phone with the restaurant and reassured me that everything was fine for Thursday. I cannot remember if we had any other conversation. We definitely did not talk about The Bitch because I am pretty sure that she was not with me at that moment.

'Oh dear', he says.

You don't have to be a rocket scientist to guess where this conversation is going. The guy gives his keyboard another short workout, and then he does something very odd. He tells me that it was impossible to get into the restaurant, and by way of illustration he holds up a clutch of notes, names and phone numbers of people who are hoping for last-minute cancellations, poor buggers who are desperate to get in, so desperate that they ignore the odds against this actually happening in a place with an eight-month waiting list, which in the end is as stupid as doing the family budget by buying a single lottery ticket and then being taken aback – shocked and taken aback – because the scheme has not worked out. I mean you can only feel sorry for such people a little bit.

I am struggling to comprehend the connection between those losers and me, because they are hoping, against colossal odds, for a reservation, and I got one. To my mind that is a huge difference, but maybe I got something wrong here and the whole thing needs to be explained to me very carefully.

He calls the restaurant, and I can tell that they are having a completely pointless, pro-forma conversation. He rings off and looks at me:

'I am sorry, sir, they have no room for you. Could I book you somewhere else, maybe?'

I want to turn on him and grab his lapels, drag him over the counter, bang his head on the marble top and start screaming at him: BOOK ME SOMEWHERE ELSE? ARE YOU OUT OF YOUR TINY FUCKING MIND? IN ONE FELL SWOOP YOU DESTROYED ALL MY ILLUSIONS ABOUT THIS JOINT. I HAVE FRIENDS ARRIVING IN UNDER AN HOUR, AND YOU ARE DOING THIS TO ME? DO YOU COMPREHEND THAT I WILL NEVER AGAIN FEEL SECURE ABOUT THIS PLACE, YOU MORON, but I don't.

I am at the end of my tether. Having been brainwashed over the last week or so into subscribing to the mantra that this is one of the greatest, best-run, bla-bla-bla hotels on the planet, nay, in the universe, it now turns out to be just as sloppily organised as the most pathetic Travelodge franchise. I am reeling with pain and disbelief. After all this it turns out that the people in charge here are just as boring and unreliable and witless as the rest of us. I cannot get over it.

They can rip out a marble bath and replace it with a jacuzzi and do the same thing again a few days later in reverse: unplumbed, rip out, replace, disconnect, refit the jacuzzi, make up all the fiddly bits, reconnect, install the electrics, re-tile, re-paint, re-grout. All this should probably earn them a place in the *Guinness Book of Records* and probably has, but I cannot be arsed to check. All this is done because Britney has run out of other ways to be impossible. Has not somebody worked out by now that all she really wants is for all this not to happen. She is provoking a rejection that somehow never comes, and all this has morphed into a reputation that she is an absolute monster bitch, when all she wants is to hear somebody say:

'No Britney, absolutely not.'

or, just to be on the safe side:

駄目だよ、**あゆみ**！絶対駄目。

or:

'Nein, Britney, nein.'

or:

'Non, Britney, absolument non.'

She would be so happy. But somehow tragically, by some weird statistical fluke it has never happened, and now of course all this has become self-fulfilling prophecy and nobody dares to say it to her and the bad reputation grows. She does not really deserve this, but there you go.

So they do all this for Britney without missing a single detail, deliver the whole thing on time – I don't think budget could have been much of an issue – and they then cannot keep their eyes on a piece of paper that says that three people will arrive six days hence at such and such a time for some food and a bottle of wine, or whatever other method they use in here to record such things. I say that they somehow got their priorities wrong. Big time.

We leave the desk and turn to the lift. The Bitch does her belly-on-the-black-and-white-marble-floor shtick, and I want to kick her and tell that there is a time and place for everything and that this is most definitely not it. We get into the lift and up to the room.

As the lift rises to the second floor I am staring at the mosaic floor, ready to burst into tears. Suddenly to my inner eye the whole edifice of Claridge's comes crashing down, a tumbling mess of six floors and 257 suites and rooms, slowly collapsing onto itself in a low, menacing rumble, the cake and sandwich stands in the lobby, two miles of corridors, the marble bathrooms, countless flower arrangements, the lift, the chandeliers, the sweeping staircase, acres of specially blocked wallpaper, curtains, soft furnishings, settees, paintings, scented candles, fluffy towels, the fleet of serving trolleys, embroidered bathrobes, tens of thousands of pieces of fine bone china, acres of wall-to-wall carpeting (enough to kit out any number of football pitches) the supercilious sub-Tissot portrait of Mrs. Claridge presiding over the lobby, the Royal Suite, the gym, the Japanese red-lacquer breakfast sets, the goddamn restaurant with its eight-month waiting list, it all caves in onto itself in a deafening, mind-blowing roar, with plaster clouds billowing up and down Brook Street, shooting out at one end into the vast expanse of Hyde Park and at the other forking left and right into New Bond Street, covering the slightly disturbing, kinky sub-porn outfits for over-sexed teen girls at Victoria's Secret in white-grey concrete dust. There is a gaggle of girls (hot pants, tank tops, fake tan and big hair) standing in front of the shop crying hysterically. What, they fret, will they wear the next time they see their boyfriends? By the end of the day three of them will have been arrested on looting charges. Even the Dale Chihuly chandelier in the lobby, to my mind the only item in the whole building lacking taste and judgment, majestically comes crashing down and is efficiently pulverised into the finest glass powder, one down and several hundreds if not thousands to go in lobbies all over the world! Car alarms are blinking and hooting all over the neighbourhood. People are standing about everywhere, staring in disbelief, doubled up in pain and coughing out their lungs. Fire engines and ambulances with wailing sirens are approaching from all directions. FUCK THIS JOINT, I think. The lift stops, and I get out. I cannot believe what just happened, and I am minded to call reception and have them pack my luggage so that I can get out right away and leave this sloppy hellhole behind. I won't do it of course. I mean where else could I get a hotel reservation on a Friday evening – and in any event none of this will help me with my friends who will arrive in just about an hour. I decide to stay and to give the hotel a second chance. These people are, after all, only human, I think magnanimously.

And then things are getting much, much worse.

Walking down the corridor I decide to call Victoria and Albert (pronounced the French way, with a silent 'T'), to tell them about the fuck-up. I think it is only proper to do so; you don't want to drag them two blocks across Mayfair and then break the bad news in the lobby. They are staying at the Connaught. Swiss-Belgian, both bankers, they are the kind of people whose lives are so well organised that if you asked them about an event in nine weeks at say 4 o'clock they could tell you exactly what they will be up to, with all the details already in place. I have never worked out how they do it. Moving the Queen about is like a stoned hippie party by comparison. I mean my life is a shambolic rolling mess of details, appointments, events, and most of the time, fingers crossed, everything works sort of out, but I am always happy to learn from real professionals.

Post-operation I especially feel that Victoria and Albert are a good example to look at in order to learn a bit more about life control.

I ring their number. Victoria is delighted to hear my voice, and I quickly tell her about the lost reservation and suggest as an alternative dinner in my suite, and maybe she would like to tell me what they would like to eat. I figure that she could at this point ask for anything and that the hotel would do whatever it takes to satisfy her wishes, by way of compensation for the mess we have just been through. I set all this out in the most casual, friendly manner because all I expect is a laugh at the absurdness of the situation and that she will then tell me what she and Albert would like to eat, tell me how much she is looking forward to seeing me shortly, and ring off happily, because that is the kind of girl I think she is.

Instead she just goes 'Oh'.

She then says that she will have to talk to Albert and put me on hold. After what feels like eternity she comes back on line. Her voice sounds different.

She sounds as if she has just been crying and that she is only just managing to hold it together. In a faltering, wispy voice she begins:

'You know I have spent months of my life in Claridge's.'

I want to yell WELL YOU LUCKY BITCH, but I hold my tongue because there is something so tragic, broken-hearted and defeated to the tone of her voice that I let her continue:

'I lived in Claridge's suites for ages, and it is no longer that exciting. So maybe we should cancel?'

I am speechless. I mean what fright does a distant memory hold that makes you forgo the prospect of an exciting evening with a juicy hot-off-the-press blow-by-blow account of a medullary-thyroid-cancer episode affecting a good friend you hold dear? Believe me, I have happily set off to Pizza Express hundreds of times with the prospect of much less. I am now really curious: what have they done to the poor woman in here to unleash such terrors? Waterboarded her for hours on end in her suite's bathroom?

Thankfully she holds it together, and I gingerly suggest that maybe we could go somewhere else? What about Nobu, she whispers. She thinks though that will be difficult, and I tell her not to worry, I will try my best. I ring off and race downstairs to reception. No point calling reception, certain things are best done face-to-face.

'Here is the deal: You messed up my reservation, and this is what the people I am dining with want to do instead. Get us a table at Nobu for 7.30,' I snarl at the concierge menacingly. He doesn't miss a beat:

'No problem, sir.'

I am barely back in my room when the phone rings.

'Sir, just to confirm, you have a table for 3 at Nobu for 7.30.'

'Thank you for sorting this.'

'You are very welcome, sir.'

I ring Victoria, who is delighted.

'Wonderful, we'll see you at the restaurant in an hour or so.'

Dinner is difficult, to say the least. Victoria and Albert are clearly very cross with me. They had wanted to go to the new restaurant at Claridge's, that was the plan, and I had messed it up. Personally. This comes on top of what else had gone wrong the previous twenty-four hours: The day before they had chartered a private jet to take them to Basel to be there in time for the super-VIP preview of the annual art fair, but so many planes were flying in that theirs was put in a holding pattern above the Swiss mountains. By the time they had landed and made it to the fair, Victoria and Albert were an hour late, and ALL THE BEST THINGS HAD ALREADY BEEN SOLD TO OTHERS.

This morning their bad luck had continued. They have been on the lookout for a London home for ages, an unending saga I must listen to every time I see them. Everything they had looked at so far was wrong in one way or another, and they were on to their third property scout in six months. The latest guy seemed promising and had come up with a charming Mayfair townhouse. Albert mentions its price, and for a moment I thought I misheard. I mean you could buy a second-hand aircraft carrier for that! They had toured the house this morning, and it was yet another terrible disappointment. At about 12,000 square feet it was far too small and barely habitable. Victoria tells me this in some weird conspiratorial way, as if I would understand without difficulty why a 12,000 square foot townhouse, your fifth home, aside from places in Geneva, Hong Kong, New York and Venice, could be too small for a middle-age couple without children. I try not to burst out laughing and instead put on my most compassionate face. It's hard, and I am not sure if I am actually succeeding. Albert chimes in and in no time works himself into a lather about how difficult it is to find a decent home in London for less than £20m, and what a slum England really is and why are they even bothering. Why indeed, I wonder. He makes it sound as though they have just been kicked off the waiting list for social housing in Tower Hamlets and will have to sleep rough.

After a while I am getting fed up with the whole thing and try to change the subject. I want to talk about my cancer for a bit. I feel this is my prerogative at the moment, and people are kind enough to indulge me: they listen carefully even if they are actually bored rigid. Not Victoria and Albert, they won't have any of it. It makes them squeamish. Victoria is on her third glass of Chardonnay and is getting a little drunk. Thankfully at 9.30 sharp she indicates that she has a terrible headache and needs to go to bed. Her husband snaps his finger, and a waitress immediately comes over with the bill. Albert hands her his credit card but tells her to take off the service charge:

'We had no service.'

I want to die, but the waitress takes this in her stride. It obviously happens in here all the time. We leave the restaurant and there is a car and driver waiting to take them the two blocks to the Connaught. They do not offer me a ride, Victoria and I air-kiss good-bye, and I shake Albert's hand and thank him for dinner. They get into the limousine and drive off, without a wave or glance back. Jesus, I think, I need some new friends. I walk down Bond Street and am back at Claridge's in five minutes.

The next twenty-four hours are not easy with the hotel staff. I am trying to convey my displeasure at the mess-up with the reservation and keep communications (and tips) to a bare minimum, no more chatty hellos, just curt nods. Things are a little frosty. But what can you do, I mean obviously everybody is aware of what has happened, and everybody is trying their best to make up for it by being even more effusive and charming than usual. When I leave for Pilates the next morning it is drizzling slightly, and the two doormen on duty each hand me an umbrella! Maids, concierges and waiters likewise are falling over backward to please. How can you resist? A day later we are back to normal. Huge relief all round.

On Monday I visit Peter at the Royal Marsden. I have been called in to discuss the result of the surgery, look at the scar, discuss how I am feeling. I am feeling anxious, to tell the truth, because there is the looming prospect of six weeks of radiation, half an hour each day. I am nervous. Peter is his charming self, he looks at the scar, asks how I am getting on. I tell him a bit about my life at Claridge's. I don't dare ask questions, so I let

86

him do the talking. He finally comes to the point: the doctors have decided that radiation is not necessary, because at present there is nothing left in my neck to hit. From now on I will be monitored very carefully every three months, just in case anything moves. This is extremely reassuring. Never again for the rest of my life will anything happen to me medically without anybody noticing. I am introduced to the team; they are highly intelligent and sympathetic people. This is going to be fun, and I am going to be the talking guinea pig! It's the best science project I have ever been involved in. When I leave they must think: what a freak.

I leave the hospital in a state of dazed elation. Outside everything looks greener, bluer, sunnier than ever, and I have to remind myself to be careful when crossing Fulham Road. It would be such a waste to get run over now. I am going straight to Peter Harrington, the antiquarian bookseller. I know the shop well and I know what I am after. They have a signed first edition of *Ulysses* by James Joyce. I buy the book there and then; it costs a king's ransom. I have wanted to own one of these for ever but never had the money or nerve or both to go after it. If this isn't the moment, I figure, when is?

On the way back to the hotel I decide that I will start fundraising for the Oracle Cancer Trust. It was set up by Peter, my surgeon, in 1979, and it clearly means a lot to him. This, I figure, is the least I can do by way of thank you.

That evening there is another dinner, another couple. After the fiasco with Victoria and Albert I am understandably a little weary, but I need not worry. Jacqueline and Marc are cut from a different cloth. I have known Jacqueline for ever and am very fond of her. She and her husband are always fun, urbane, sophisticated, informed, full of curiosity. Good on politics, good on the absurdness of everyday life, wickedly funny about the art world. They are concerned about me, and much of the

evening is taken up by medical talk, private versus public, the
US system compared with Europe, how expensive it all is.
Telling me! From time to time it gets very silly, and at one point
we briefly discuss the sex lives or non-sex lives of people we
barely know, like ████████████ and ████████████.
There is no malice here, just playfulness and great relief that
I am OK.

Jacqueline talks about her children. She talks about them in
a way that used to make me madly jealous; there is a warmth
there and an engagement that has an other worldly quality.
I don't know her kids personally, but I feel I know them
through her words. I am no longer jealous. I just love to hear
her talk and watch her. The evening is a huge success. Before
we part we discuss summer plans, what will they do and where
will I be? We have an odd routine: every year I suggest an
evening at Glyndebourne, and here we are discussing it again.
Should we go this summer? He is keen, and she is not so sure, so
I guess as every year we won't go.

After dinner I take The Bitch for her evening walk. We loiter in
front of Annabel's for a while, as I am hoping for another joke.
Nothing. The doorman gives me a funny look, but I think this is
because he is misreading The Scar.

We return to the hotel and off to bed. Before I fall asleep
I realise with amazement that I have not given a fuck about The
Dog Blanket for three days. One less thing to fret about.

Oh The Scar. It is healing remarkably fast, too fast actually.
I still have the ambition to watch somebody clock it and start
puking; I think I have watched a scene like this once in a movie.
It's fading so fast that in a few weeks such a person will have to
be close, as if they were about to kiss my neck. A joke-shop scar
put on top of the actual one might extend the window of
opportunity a little longer, but can I really be bothered?

Giving The Scar the look. People are still staring at it with fascination. Very few dare to ask directly; instead there is a weird, delicate peek-a-boo ballet going on, looking, looking away, looking, looking away, looking again, until I put them out of their misery and volunteer the information. Don't worry, it's only thyroid cancer, but I am OK now. I wonder if it would help if I had a few V-neck T-shirts printed up with black lettering:

ASK THE QUESTION

or:

LOOKING FOR A FIGHT?

or:

WHAT THE FUCK ARE YOU FUCKING LOOKING AT?

or:

NO WORRY
IT IS MEDICAL

I like the third one best because it is so unambiguous. I mean you would have to be on crack to say 'The Scar'.

Now is it clearer like this:

WHAT THE FUCK ARE YOU FUCKING
LOOKING AT?

or like that:

WHAT THE FUCK
ARE YOU
FUCKING LOOKING AT?

No, it's beginning to look like an eye-test chart – and it sounds like one as well – so let's go back to:

WHAT THE FUCK ARE YOU FUCKING LOOKING AT?

Now what about colour?

WHAT THE FUCK ARE YOU FUCKING LOOKING AT?

WHAT THE FUCK ARE YOU FUCKING LOOKING AT?

WHAT THE FUCK ARE YOU FUCKING LOOKING AT?

WHAT THE FUCK ARE YOU FUCKING LOOKING AT?

WHAT THE FUCK ARE YOU FUCKING LOOKING AT?

WHAT THE FUCK ARE YOU FUCKING LOOKING AT?

WHAT THE FUCK ARE YOU FUCKING LOOKING AT?

WHAT THE FUCK ARE YOU FUCKING LOOKING AT?

WHAT THE FUCK ARE YOU FUCKING LOOKING AT?

WHAT THE FUCK ARE YOU FUCKING LOOKING AT?

Personally I like this one best:

WHAT THE FUCK ARE YOU FUCKING LOOKING AT?

In case you are colour-blind, orange is my favourite colour.

[Author's note to editor: No, I don't think we can presume that *all* readers of this book will be colour-blind and print *all the above in black*. Think about it, the odds against this are just too gigantic. I know that Finance is already fretting. The bookkeeper (Tony) is very charming, and I am sure will happily fudge the whole colour thing through without anyone noticing. If you do the layout carefully you could get all of it on one page. I am sure the designer, Tim, will be able to sort this.]

A few weeks later I have an intern research T-shirts, and it turns out that the vinyl lettering has to be at least two centimetres tall to stencil out properly, so I adapt the design as follows:

front   back

While the intern is at it he also makes up a mouse-mat prototype, an iPhone cover and a mug. Before the novel is even finished we have the whole promotional product line in place! I am particularly pleased with the mouse mat and use it all the time. The T-shirt samples disappear in no time. Everybody wants one.

The next morning Sarah arrives for breakfast.

She is a bit shaken by events at home over the last few days. A 'friend' of hers had left her in charge of a black schnauzer (aged 2) named Rigby. I personally don't think Sarah is a natural with animals, and I would never leave The Bitch in her care, but other people can of course do with their pets whatever they like. I don't think that there was anything fundamentally wrong with Rigby; he was just a little confused about being in a new environment, taken care of by a person that obviously has a problem with dogs (or animals in general). He sounded actually rather cute, with his schnauzer fringe and waggy little tail.

Sarah complained that Rigby was following her about the house. She would find him waiting for her outside the toilet. She would tiptoe off the sofa to the kitchen so that Rigby would not wake up, but she inevitably failed. She complained that when Rigby peed 'the hair around his penis would drip with urine'. She noted that 'his anus was dirty' after he had taken a shit and that 'he wasn't doing anything about this'. I wonder what exactly she was expecting him to do? Use a bidet? As far as I remember she doesn't have one in her bathroom. Does she expect the dog to go next door and use her neighbours'? Do they actually have one? Would Sarah ring the doorbell for him, or does she imagine Rigby to stand on his hind legs and push the button on his own? What a weird idea. She was minded to take wet wipes to the park to deal with this 'hygiene issue' herself. Apparently she also had started wiping Rigby's paws on entering the house in case he had stepped into urine. I cannot remember if she was talking about his urine or the urine of other dogs, and I think that she probably did not make a rational distinction between the two. The owner collected Rigby last night. I hope this is true, and that the poor mutt did not end up crammed into Sarah's freezer. We all know how brutal and irrational really crazy people can become. I was shocked by all this, especially the bit about the 'dripping penis'; I mean you would have to take a pretty close look to notice things like that. Revelations of this kind are always upsetting. I had Sarah down as one of my mentally stronger friends. How could I have guessed that she was actually one of the more disturbed loonies in my circle?

We are about to leave the suite when she suddenly shrieks in the entrance lobby. The British Museum cake has started oozing gunk all over the lobby table. This looks interesting, and I wonder what kind of cake it actually is. Fruit? Nut? Fruit and nut? I cannot explore further because I have to keep Sarah calm. I immediately cover the whole thing with a napkin to stop her from completely losing her composure. Thankfully at this very moment a hotel maid walks in to collect the breakfast stuff, and I beg her to remove the cake. Thank God the trolley is in the room. How did they know about the impending cake situation, or was the latest disobedience of my trolley veto and the cake business just a happy coincidence? I am sorry that I was not able to save the marzipan photo image of The Bitch, but it would have been a messy affair and not worth the bother. Have you noticed that nobody ever eats photos printed on sheet marzipan? They always get thrown out. It would be much easier if they were printed on plastic so you could keep them as a souvenir without mess. Note to self: remember to write thank-you to British Museum gang telling them how much I enjoyed the cake and how delicious it was.

[Author's note: Before the cake went off I had taken pictures of it on my phone to be used on the book cover. When Tim, the designer, three months later looked at these they turned out to be out-of-focus and of no use. With the help of the British Museum people we were able to have the cake remade and professionally photographed. This time around we ate it for tea at the office. It was actually delicious.]

I surreptitiously text my friends at David Zwirner Gallery, telling them that I am in the midst of a real emergency and can I please drop off The Bitch at their reception. At first they fear that it is something to do with The Scar. I assure them no and say that I will explain later.

We park The Bitch at the gallery (they love her there at reception) and head for the National Gallery to look at Cézanne's *Large Bathers*, which as you already know is one of my favourite paintings. The moment we have dropped The Bitch Sarah stops babbling and perspiring. It is obviously dogs (Rigby and The Bitch) or images of dogs (the marzipan image of the latter) that affect her very badly. I should alert all our mutual friends to this.

Thankfully Sarah has calmed down, though I can tell that she is still on the lookout for dogs and constantly scans her surroundings. On our way to the National Gallery we stop at Connaught Brown on Albemarle Street. Sarah says that you never know what you find there. I know the owner, Anthony. He is one of those old-fashioned dealers who ferrets out interesting things and actually enjoys what he is doing. Sarah makes her own round through the gallery and then calls me excitedly from a small side room. Oh no, I think, not a picture of a dog. Instead she stands in front of a small early landscape painting by Piet Mondrian. It's a little jewel, a grey, low Hague School sky, a Cézanne-esque foreground with a turning road and in the middle a group of gabled farmhouses. On the barn are at least four little squares, the barn door and three shuttered windows. I am not saying that it is a straight line from this to *Victory Boogie-Woogie* [1942–44], but there is something here: a supreme painterly intelligence at its outset, trying to figure things out, trying to establish a way of working that suits the artist's temperament. The picture has a presence that is out of proportion to both its size and modest ambition. The paint handling is confident and loose, already no longer completely in the service of representation. The squares on the barn are something else. The little painting is pure magic. Sarah and I silently admire it. Finally we turn to reception and ask the young man behind it for some information and the price. He is clearly nervous, maybe he is new to the job but I fear that it may have to do with Sarah's and my appearance. Sarah remains twitchy and looks, to be honest, certifiably mad, and I, well, I've got The Scar and the bloody snot dribbling down my front. He is on his own and anxious, still, he is trying his best. He engages us in a conversation, gives us background information and tells us that the painting is signed with Mondrian's pre-Paris signature:

'There are two A's,' he helpfully points out.

Sarah is not having any of it and gets rather snappy. I get the price out of him, the painting is an absolute bargain. I tell him that I would like to reserve it and that I will talk to Anthony on Monday. The mention of his boss's name reassures him a little. In case you are wondering, what I am spending on the signed Joyce *Ulysses* AND The Little Mondrian would not buy a Dale Chihuly ashtray. My choices are obviously clear.

We have barely left the gallery when Sarah breaks into a furious rage.

'How dare he. I mean "two A's" – does he think we can't count? What a patronizing little shit!'

'Oh come on, Sarah, he was only making polite conversation.' I am actually not so sure, I think the kid clocked the situation, got unnerved and threw us a puzzle:

'Can you see the two A's in Mondriaan?'

As we were trying to figure it out, ONE, TWO, he would have enough time to get to the phone and dial 999.

We finally make it to the National Gallery. Sarah wants to look at the COLOUR exhibition. It is unbelievably boring. Do the curators really believe that all their visitors are moronic half-wits?

We leave the basement and head upstairs to look at Cézanne's *Large Bathers*. There is a bench in front of the painting, and Sarah and I sit down. The longer you look at *The Bathers* the stranger it becomes. It eludes comprehension. One tourist after another plants himself between the picture and us.

'Do these people all believe they are translucent?' I ask Sarah.

Another backpacker rocks up. I want to scream at him but don't. 'And have you noticed that the fatter they are the more translucent they believe themselves to be?'

It is impossible to look at the Cézanne without continuous disruption. Every twenty-odd seconds another fat person moves in front of us, so we finally give up and leave the museum. I escort Sarah to the nearest tube station and say good-bye and head back to Mayfair. I want to have another look at The Little Mondrian. I have not been so excited about any art purchase for myself for quite some time and need to have another look. I stop by at David Zwirner's to collect The Bitch. She is actually pleased to see me. When we get to Albemarle Street, Connaught Brown is shut. Strange, I think, it is only 4.30. Well, maybe the kid was so freaked out by Sarah and me that he turned off the lights, locked up and went home – who can blame him? I return to Claridge's via Bond Street, still gridlocked with Bentleys and pedestrians. The lobby is heaving with exhausted shoppers.

Three hours later I phone Sarah to find out if she has gotten home. I find her hysterical and pretty much incoherent. It takes fifteen minutes to calm her down. She cannot actually explain why she is in such a state. I invite her for dinner next Wednesday. I have to give repeat assurances that The Bitch will not be here. Our mutual friend Antonia kindly agrees to join us. All this is very upsetting. At what time does one get social services involved? Is there an anonymous phone-in line, or does one need to make an appointment in person? What is the etiquette,

I wonder? Should I call Sarah's daughters? How will they cope?

Too much time in Mayfair gives you delusions of grandeur, or maybe it's just still a side effect from the painkillers; anyway, yesterday I went to Smythson to order bookplates. For some bizarre reason I thought that this would be a great idea, something I really needed, and I ordered 2,000 red ones and 2,000 orange ones, bordered in the same colours:

and

I have to say that the shop assistant was not particularly forthcoming. Though I dropped a hint that I have been a client for three decades (note cards), she made her own judgment based on The Scar and my slightly dishevelled appearance. The Scar is still oozing a bit, and I am also still a bit woozy, so the overall impression is still not exactly sharp. She may also have thought that four thousand bookplates was a bit excessive, not to say plain mad. Anyway, she made a huge speech about how she needed advance payment, I gave her my email address, asked her to send her invoice and assured her that payment would be with them by the following morning – and this was the last I ever heard. I am glad because what a potential disaster! I mean somebody would have to glue all these plates into my books! Some poor intern would be busy for months on end! How would he decide which colour plate to put where? By genre (in which case we would have to order a few other colours)? Or alternate orange and red from book to book, down the shelves? Or maybe by mood? As it would have to be my mood (because who cares about his? In any event, doing this job his mood would consistently be dark), he would have to call me every time he were about to place a plate in a book:

'Uh, hello, sorry for disturbing you again, but what colour bookplate would you like me to place in Nancy J Troy's *The Afterlife of Piet Mondrian*?'

'That's a tricky one, I would say off the top of my head orange but maybe red would be better? Can I call you back about this?'

'Sure.'

'Maybe we should look at all the other books on Mondrian and see what we have done so far?'

'I will have a look and report back to you on this.'

'Thanks.'

'Bye.'

'Bye.'

He would then have to look at all the Mondrian books on my

London shelves and then get a train from King's Cross to Norfolk and a cab from the station to the cottage so that he can check the Mondrian books there too. He would never get anything done. What a complete farce, and expensive too! As you can see we would not get much gluing done. In reality the boxes of plates would clutter up my flat for a few months, to be moved to storage and later deep storage, never to be seen again, until some other, future intern took mercy and threw them out, without even asking me about it. Just like that.

I used to love Smythson. It was a slightly fusty stationery emporium, and it made me quite nervous to go in and file my annual note-card order (I still file the same order once a year). The place had real attitude, and they liked to make you feel like an impostor. The assistants were of a certain age, wore twin sets and had cut-glass accents. Like all of Bond Street, Smythson has changed. It now looks like a set for a new Tim Burton movie in which we see a wild-haired Helena Bonham Carter staggering through an interminable maze of candy-coloured handbags, clutches, wallets, and credit-card holders. I know all this must be good taste because the Prime Minister's wife is running the company, but still. All that stuff is menacingly closing in on poor Helena; she is shrieking and panting and can't find her way out of the maze. Who, pray, buys all this? Whenever I am in there the leather goods department is empty of customers. It takes for ever to get through it all to get to the stationery counter at the back. Every time I go in I think heretically DO I REALLY WANT TO BUY MY NOTE CARDS FROM A PLACE THAT SELLS ALL THIS CANDY-COLOURED CRAP? Inevitably I come back for my next order.

   A thought: all the leather goods from one end of Bond Street to the other look the same. Maybe everything is produced in one location, and different logos are stapled, glued or stitched on at the very last minute, on delivery. This is sort of what

I always suspect happens across town at Camden Lock: all these funky indie stalls are all somehow centrally supplied from a single warehouse somewhere in central China. Not possible? How can you be so sure? Have you been to China and checked? Something similar to Camden Lock is happening on Bond Street, just at a much higher price point.

The book is progressing at the most alarming rate (right off the proliferation chart). I have to pace myself. I mean I don't want it to become known as the *War and Peace* of cancer novels. Nobody would read it. Nobody probably will anyway.

There are notes strewn all over the sitting room, and sometimes I cannot keep up with writing things down as they happen. I wish I had shorthand.

The next morning a pageboy delivers a package. It contains a very beautiful brown cashmere blanket, a very generous cheque made out to Oracle Cancer Trust and a note that reads as follows:

Dear

With much love,

I am deeply touched.

[Excerpt from The Diary of The Political Prisoner, Room 212]
This place is definitely going to hell. After all these years
they still cannot get my breakfast order straight: EARL
GREY TEA, BROWN TOAST, STRAWBERRY JAM, ON A
TROLLEY. What is there not to get? I wonder. This morning
they brought DARJEELING TEA, WHITE TOAST, APRICOT
JAM ON A TRAY. Sometimes I think they do this on purpose
to wind me up. Staff should know by now that I cannot
stand TRAYS, I think they are very common. Still, I should
not complain. Had I made it to the Ecuadorian Embassy
I would by now be sharing with Julian Assange. I hear that
the guy is a creep and that the embassy is a frightful dump.
Assange sleeps on a makeshift bed in the ambassador's
study. He has to do his own laundry and cooking…]

Wednesday: Dinner with Sarah and Antonia. I make a special
effort, rearrange the ushabtis, order fresh flowers. I toy with the
idea of candles but desist. I mean what a nightmare for the
hotel people, can you imagine two hundred rooms with candles
and careless guests? Things are already bad enough with over-
flowing baths. I have The Little Mondrian just for the evening.
The gallery won't let me have it for good because it is part of
their summer group show, so a pageboy collects it from
Albemarle Street just before 6 and another pageboy will deliver
it back in the morning.

Sarah arrives at 7.30 sharp. Before I let her in I lock The
Bitch in the bedroom. I offer Sarah a glass of Krug, which she
happily accepts. Pouring the drink I surreptitiously drop in a
Diazepam. The champagne fizzes up, and the pill dissolves
instantly. She happily drinks down her glass, and I offer her
another. Antonia arrives a few minutes later. We have a look
round the suite, and The Little Mondrian is much admired. We
talk about this and that, the way it is when good friends come
together. I let The Bitch out of the bedroom, and Sarah does not

even notice. Dinner is served. Much of the conversation is about Mougouch, Antonia's mother and a dear friend of Sarah's and mine. She died a year ago. Only a few months earlier Sarah and I had taken Mougouch to Paris. She was wonderful, we looked at museums, visited a Cézanne exhibition at the Musée du Luxembourg, and had a memorable dinner at the Voltaire, to my mind the most elegant restaurant in town. Mougouch had insisted that we walk absolutely everywhere, it was utterly exhausting but she could not get enough. She was an indomitable spirit, kind, funny and engaging, and she never complained about anything, even when she was ill and feeling low. I realise that I learned so much from her over the years, and I like to think that she would have approved of the way I have dealt with things over the last few months. She would definitely have enjoyed the whole Claridge's episode and visited often. I miss her.

I brag to a New York friend about the signed *Ulysses* first edition. A few days later an Amazon package arrives from the States. In it is a copy of a new book, *The Most Dangerous Book* by Kevin Birmingham, about the publishing history of Joyce's masterpiece. There is also a printed card:

> **'A gift from** ▮▮▮▮▮▮▮▮▮
> **Good health!**
> **Enjoy your gift!**
> **Love, Molly'**

Lunch with ▮▮▮▮. Lots of political gossip. Apparently if you work for the Labour Shadow Attorney General you have to sign a confidentiality agreement and swear to reveal nothing, ever. What would there be to reveal? This is either delusion of grandeur, or maybe somebody forgot to tell the Labour top brass that they had actually lost the last election?

This morning Boris Johnson had said that Tony Blair was mad. I am an instant Johnson convert (for the day at least), but how many more intelligent people does it take to state the same before lazy journalists stop taking Tony Blair's calls? Why can't the Blairs just take all their millions and depart to Switzerland, quietly? Instead he keeps rubbing our nose in it.

Hard to believe, apparently Euan Blair is in the frame for a Labour safe seat with a majority of 20,000. This sure is proof that shamelessness is genetically predisposed.

I have paid for The Little Mondrian and visit Anthony at his gallery. He tells me again that I cannot have the painting until August because it is part of his summer group show. I point out to him that the show is not, strictly speaking, 'curated' but just a group of things.

'Ouch. You really know how to hurt a guy.'

Still, he lets me take the picture, and it now sits on the mantle in my sitting room. I cannot stop looking at it.

A note arrives from Pauline. She is a dear old friend, and what she writes is full of compassion and deeply touching. We should see more of each other, she always says. We never do.

Afternoon nap.

6

Dream within a dream: I am Brooke Astor, I am in my apartment on Fifth Avenue, diagonally opposite the Metropolitan Museum of Art. I am 104 years old. I have just realised that my son, Tony, age 82, has, without my permission, sold my favourite painting, The Little Mondrian. It used to hang above the marble fireplace in my library. In its place he has put a framed colour photograph of Dale Chihuly in front of the chandelier he had just finished for Claridge's in London. The photo is dedicated, 'To Brooke, affectionately from Dale Chihuly'. He gave it to me because he tried to manipulate me into using my influence as a trustee of the New York Public Library to commission one of his 'works' for the library's Fifth Avenue entrance lobby. I wanted to tell him YOU MUST BE JOKING – I DON'T EVEN CALL WHAT YOU ARE DOING 'ART' but I didn't. The photo ended up in the maid's bedroom, where Tony must have found it. Does my son really think that I cannot tell the difference between a Mondrian and a photo with an insincere dedication? Come on, Tony, I may be 104 but I am not gaga!

When Tony comes to visit I have a word with him about the missing painting:
'I really want The Little Mondrian back, Tony. It was absolutely not yours to sell.'

'Mother. Please. We mustn't have this conversation in front of the staff.'

I cannot begin to convey to you how angry I am. I open my eyes.

I am in a cold sweat, blindly tugging at my single strand of natural pearls.

I wake up with a start, nervously clawing at The Scar, and then I realise to my horror that I am holding a chunky piece of scab between my fingers. What a weird dream!

[Excerpt from The Diary of The Political Prisoner, Room 212] 'Overheard conversation between doorman and concierge in lobby yesterday, apparently there is a publishing big shot from Random House in Room 225-6, entertaining in his suite day and night, the traffic never stops. Rumour has it that he is giving a fancy party in a few days' time somewhere in North London. I have seen the guy several times in the corridor; he could have fooled me. I mean he does not look like a big shot; he looks frightful actually, with that ugly scar on his neck. It's so off-putting, why can't he wear a cravat to spare us the sight? And what about his shirt-front – must he really blow his nose on it – and that scruffy little terrier that shuffles after him? If I had a say they would ban dogs from Claridge's, especially small, ugly ones. Still, as we all know you can no longer judge people by their appearance. I have to find a way to get an invitation to his party. I want to find a publisher for my diaries and what better way to start the search than in a roomful of people in publishing? And I read somewhere that Random House pays well.'

Coming home from dinner I am startled to find the weird guy from Room 212 loitering in front of my door. Could he have a word? Reluctantly I let him in and offer a drink.
'Japanese whisky?'
    'Oh yes, please.'
He takes the glass and gulps the stuff down like he hasn't had a drink for ages.

'Another?'

'Yes.'

The Bitch does not like the man and growls. I tell her to shut it, and she skulks off to the bedroom.

The guy then cuts to the chase. He has heard that I was about to host a publishing party and was there a chance that I could invite him? He is happy to pay. I am a little taken aback by this, on several counts: One, nobody has ever offered money to get an invitation from me. Some people claim that they would rather pay than attend one of my parties, but that's another story. Two, what makes this scruffy, pasty-looking guy think that I actually sell invitations? He senses my hesitation:

'I'll give you £100'

Three, does he really think that I am that cheap? But then I have an amusing idea: I could give his £100 to the Oracle Cancer Trust. And what harm could the guy possibly be? I mean my flat will be packed with noisy, drunken people who all know each other. He will feel completely out of place and probably leave after an hour or so. And who knows, he might turn out to be rather fun, though I doubt it. He looks deeply troubled and miserable.

'OK, give me the £100 now, and you are invited!'

He holds his glass out in such a manipulative way that I pour him another double whisky. He drinks it down in three gulps and puts the glass down.

'Let me get the money. I will be right back.'

He leaves the room and comes back a few minutes later. I can hear The Bitch growling softly from the dark of the bedroom.

'Here is the money.'

He counts out four £20 notes and puts down a handful of coins.

'Great. I'll make sure that your name is with the doorman on the invitation list. Let me give you the address.'

He hesitates:

'No. I want a proper invitation. In writing.'

'Uh?'

'I. Want. It. In. Wri-ting.'

I am minded to tell him to take his money and fuck off, but I don't. Instead I assure him that he will receive an invitation tomorrow morning, to his room, and that he need not worry about his £100. He knew, after all, where he could find me. I can tell that he is not happy with all this but there you go. 'You can of course just take your money, and we leave it at that.'

He picks up his empty glass emphatically, and I pour him another drink.

He gulps down the whisky and without a word leaves my room. God, some people have no manners! Before I go to bed I count the money: £96. I can't believe it, the little shit short-changed me.

[Excerpt from The Diary of The Political Prisoner, Room 212]
'Last night had talk with the Random House guy. We had drinks in his suite, very fancy, books and flowers everywhere. There is a small painting by Mondrian on the mantle, not bad but far too early. On his writing desk a row of ushabtis, which is a bit creepy. Still, he invited me to his publishing party. A pageboy delivers the invitation this morning, addressed to 'Room 212'. I had forgotten to give the Random House guy my name. I tell the pageboy to wait while I rummage for some change. Money is in short supply, the embassy again has 'forgotten' my quarterly remittance. I give him 50p, which he pockets with a derisory snort. I hate pageboys; they are insolent, arrogant and expensive. Still, things are definitely looking up. If I play my cards right at the Random House party I could be an international publishing sensation by next spring!'

A deeply disturbing note is received in Room 225-6:

'Darling –
[1] How very sad I was to hear of this terrible sickness, what a shock.
[…] [2] We run around thinking of material possessions.
[…] [3] I always remember that lovely dinner you gave for
████████████.' [There follows a lot of personal stuff best left unexposed, and the letter closes with the statement that] [4] 'life knocks you over and then the reality becomes real. […]'

Here are my observations: [1] Personally I would not talk to a person that has just been through major cancer surgery about 'terrible sickness' and 'shock'. It's tactless. [2] Don't include me here. This is exclusively your problem and always has been. [3] The dinner she is talking about took place a quarter of a century ago. Since then she has invited me for dinner once. She has never been to my home, has not set foot into my gallery – so what is she on about? [4] '…and then the reality becomes real': well, that's just mad, plain and simple. The note is actually sinister and I bin it.

The next evening another couple – Andrew and Ingrid – comes over for dinner. He is a curator at Tate Britain; she runs her own not-for-profit art space, PEER in Shoreditch. The evening is a great success. They are sweet, charming, intelligent and funny. We talk about the usual subjects: politics, the absurdness of the art world, nothing too heavy – deep down we are enchanted with it and love what we are doing professionally. We talk about my cancer, naturally. We also talk about the novel, and I read them a few scenes from the first draft. They 'get it' right away and make some very useful suggestions. I explain the multiple-voice, post-modern conceit, the forays into Mayfair, the shopping critique, The Little Mondrian, the KGB station in the basement, the jacuzzi, The Bitch, The Political Prisoner. We have two bottles of the mystery claret over dinner and finish off with shots of Japanese whisky. They finally leave at midnight, and I walk them round the corner to their car, a clapped-out Peugeot 205, with one door (blue) replaced but never repainted to match. It always seems fine in north London, but round here it looks abandoned and burned out. The Bitch and I carry on to Berkeley Square. Back at the hotel in the corridor to our room she falls back and when I turn round to call her she is peeing in the middle of the carpet, a little warning for the white poodle! I race to the room to get some loo-paper to dab up the piss. We will of course have been captured by at least two security cameras pointing from either end of the corridor. Thankfully it is late, and nobody else has appeared. I shoo The Bitch into the suite. Was this really necessary, I chide her. It is quite obvious that she couldn't care less. I call Andrew and leave a message, telling him what just happened. Text exchange:

> Just a thought but won't the KGB cameras have picked up The Bitch's transgression on the corridor carpet? Could provide a good sequence for the movie perhaps?
> Thanks for tonight – a lot of fun!

> Yawn thought of this already.

> Well – that's post-post-modernity for you.

In the novel when describing the scene I will move the pee-stain about fifteen yards down the corridor, right in front of Room 212. Serves him right.

The weather is glorious. I phone Mandana, and we meet with the dogs in Green Park. Her friend Jane and her dog are joining us.

Jane and Mandana are long-standing Soho residents who are down-to earth and very practical. Jane runs a restaurant, and Mandana is in charge of a members' club, and you have to be switched-on to do these things successfully. They talk Soho politics, and I join the conversation, partly because my office is in Soho, and I am genuinely interested in what is going on round there but also for selfish reasons. Talking to these women will prepare me for the return to 'civilian' life after my time at Claridge's. For this, I figure, I will need all the help I can get.

Soho apparently has been 'discovered' by Russians who are fleeing capital from Moscow and parking it in London. Mandana is incensed, she was OK with it all as long as it was happening in Mayfair, but now the tidal wave of money is seeping across Regent Street into Soho. This is how it works: say in Russia you have $100 million which you need to get out pronto. The money isn't quite accounted for, and Putin could be after you any time. So you set up a chain of offshore entities, bank accounts, family trusts, Swiss bank accounts and whatnots, push the money through and spend all of it on London real estate. It is so complicated, long-winded and boring, and so hard to trace, that even you yourself might lose track of your own money. You then sell the property, and even if you were to take a hit and lose, say, half of it you will still be happy. $50 million of ill-gotten gains in London is much better than $100 million of the same stuff in Moscow. You only need to look at Putin and Cameron to understand the difference. Putin might go after you, and he would not concern himself much with legal niceties. Cameron would never, ever go after you, however bad you may stink. Still, the whole laundering process is tedious and time-consuming. I suggest an alternative solution:

'How about a whole floor at Claridge's? Wouldn't that about take care of half of it in a reasonable time frame? You then offer Britney a consulting contract, say $2m. She will come up with a series of stupid and expensive ideas, to be executed by the charming and patient hotel staff. If you are in a hurry and don't want to look too arty, repeat her jacuzzi idea in every bathroom on your floor. Have them take bathtubs out and put jacuzzis in and take jacuzzis out and put bathtubs in until the money has disappeared. All of it. I am not that good at maths but I am pretty sure $50m will be gone in no time. It's not very elegant or original but definitely efficient, and it will be fun to watch for a bit at least. There is the added advantage that even a future Labour government won't be able to go after you because there will really be no money left. Anywhere. Personally I don't think they would do anything anyway. Still, this is politics, and weirder stuff has happened. Anyway, your problem would be solved: there would be no money left either in Moscow or London. Magic!'

The girls look at me in a funny way.

The conversation moves to the subject of grocery shopping in Soho:

'You know they are about to close the Co-op store in Brewer Street?

'Oh what a shame. So where are you going now?'

'There is a Sainsbury's in Wardour Street but it is not very good.'

'How about Tesco's near Tottenham Court Rd?

'Oh no, I can't stand it, every Tom, Dick and Harry shops there.'

None of this means anything to me but I want to make a contribution.

'Well, you can always go to Fortnum and Mason on Piccadilly.'

Mandana is a good friend. She knows I am struggling with reality, but she does not want to discourage:

'That would be OK in the morning but you would have problems in the evening.'
'Why?'
'They shut at nine.'
I think I am catching the drift. I beam:
'Well if all fails there is always room service at Claridge's. It's twenty-four hours!'
Another funny look. I give up.

My phone rings. It's Maddy from my office. She tells me a terrible story about her son Frank, aged five. He arrived home yesterday screaming and covered in blood. There was so much blood that she could not tell where it was coming from. It turns out that he caught his finger in a gate and all he was left with was bare bone! The poor kid was about to go into shock, so she raced him to A & E. There was a long queue – you know the kind of people clogging up emergency rooms everywhere, a sort of free entertainment for the fat, bored and lonely. She bowled them out of the way, I wish I had been there to see it – she is so good at that sort of thing. The doctors managed to save the finger. What a terrible saga. Poor little Frank.

I call Sarah to find out how she is doing. What a relief; she is much better and sounds positively normal. What are her plans? She is excited:
'I am going to a Bach concert at lunchtime!'
I am so relieved, she is her pretentious little self again! I am so happy. Let's hope it will last and she won't suffer a relapse. Still, I am nervous about her long-term prognosis.

The New Brown Blanket looks great next to the old Dog Blanket, one on the left-hand side of my bed and the other on the right-hand side. I have been back to the bedroom only four times this morning and switched blankets from left to right to left to right and to left again. Somehow the new arrangement does not work either way, though I find it hard to pinpoint why there is a problem. Still, I am fairly relaxed about the whole business. I mean we have a whole week to figure things out.

Doro told me that I was overheard in the lobby saying to one of the hotel staff that I was fed up with 'the whole novel shit'. This place is such a gossip den! Somebody misheard. The doorman and I were having a conversation about literary form and creativity. What I was saying about my present work was that as an author you know from instinct when you are done: your job is done when your feeling of writing creatively turns into the boredom of typing. The word 'shit' never came up.

I still have the nagging fear that this book might be perceived as too short, and here is my reply to this: frankly if you don't get this joke after 120-odd pages (novella) then 300 pages (novel) won't help you much either, and I don't think things would improve at all if I pumped this up to Proustian scale, quite the opposite actually. As an author you need to know when to stop naturally.

I am tempted to give the Oracle Cancer Trust the film rights to this book. Who would I like to see play myself? I think Kevin Spacey. Doro: Helena Bonham Carter? Mandana: Kirsten Scott Thomas? Sarah: Julianne Moore? Britney should definitely be asked to play herself. It will be expensive, but they could always save money by buying the jacuzzi footage from the BBC, rather than having the whole thing restaged at Claridge's. [Author to editor: Can you please have one of the interns flesh this out. I don't go to the movies much so I need some help here. Who are the current 'hot stars', I want to give this passage an 'in-the-know' quality.] It would be quite a demanding project, and it would inevitably come out a dog's dinner. Still, if the money became really serious and bought Peter, say, a whole new wing for his hospital, I would swallow my authorial pride and go along with it. It would be easy – I just won't go to see the film. Anyway, surely nobody would dare accuse me of selling out when it is for charity? Well, we all know how mean and jealous people can be.

Still, the idea of the movie worries me. I can always build in a poison defence, like the novel could only be filmed if Kevin Spacey played my part. That would surely stop it from happening. He is a highly intelligent man who would recognise right away that this turkey could never fly.

The Bitch is being difficult. Having flat-out refused the beautiful and well-maintained Claridge's dog basket we had to ship, all the way from Kentish Town, by Addison Lee car service, her beat-up wine crate that she prefers to sleep in, with its skanky Ridinghouse-bag covered cushion, made by a friend of Antonio's as a sort of office in-joke and long overdue for a wash. Who does The Bitch think she is? Britney? The Bitch is clearly having enough of the whole Claridge's spiel. Every time I walk past the wine crate she (The Bitch, not Britney) looks at me like she is about to die of boredom and gives one of those meaningful deep sighs. What a manipulative little bitch (The Bitch, not Britney, come on reader, concentrate). Anyway she needs to be careful. I won't have her ruin my last week. If she carries on like this maybe Maddy should take her back to Dorset for the weekend and her son, Frank, might find her company amusing while he is recovering from his dreadful injury.

I am still worried that the book will be too short. I mean we have probably only six reasonably good jokes here, maximum, and you can repeat these only so often. If there really is a problem we could always extend my conversation with Dylan by another ten pages or so, ditto the T-shirt list. This, by the way, is neither creative writing nor typing but cut-and-paste and can be done by the designer, Tim.

I would love to be there when the returns come in at Hatchards on Piccadilly. Imagine English type in tweeds, posh voice, slightly querulous, a little accusatory, as if he really thinks that the bookshop assistant had personally screwed up:

'Excuse me sir, there is something wrong with the book I bought last week: thirty pages have been bound in error in multiples and another eight are blank.'

The Hatchards man does not say anything, he just looks in the English guy's direction and then – wham! The best of the staff are so good at this, you can't even work out where it is coming from, a split-second facial thing that screams OH FOR GOODNESS SAKE, YOU LITTLE SAD HOME COUNTY MORON, IT'S MEANT TO BE LIKE THIS.

He then offers something in exchange he considers more up to the poor man's speed, like a Jeffrey Archer paperback or the new Nigella cookery book.

7

I am halfway through our stay at Claridge's, and there is melancholy in the air. The Bitch is sensing it too. I get up at 7 and take her for a short walk round the block. When we come back to the hotel, she lets herself be dragged across the marble floor of the lobby in what I consider her best performance yet. We share the lift with an American who immediately strikes up a conversation about border terriers. We get to our room, and I order breakfast.

'Good morning sir, will this be the usual?'
'Yes please.'
'Darjeeling tea, toast and apricot jam?'
'Yes please.'
'Very well, sir.'
I want a glass of orange juice too, but that would have meant breaking the spell, and I desist. By this time I am a tear-eyed, snot-dripping sentimental wreck and take a look at the front page of the *Financial Times*.

I need not have worried about ordering the orange juice and breaking the spell because the paper's masthead is doing so with assassin-like precision anyway. It says there:

Don't blame me. Tony Blair, Page 11

I read it again, carefully, word for word, just to make sure. And then things get worse. The butler opens the door and brings in my breakfast on a trolley. At this moment I am ready to pass out. You can't put a guy through all this in the space of only a few minutes, but here it is happening: Tony and the trolley at the same time, a cruel, out-of-the-blue double whammy, unprovoked and from nowhere.

I can't even be bothered to read what Tony has to say for himself because we have all heard it so many times before. I mean asking Tony about Iraq is about as predictable as asking Sarah about dogs – why bother? You know what either will say, but it is also unkind to rile them. To my mind it is wrong to consciously provoke a mad person into a rage, and it makes no difference if they are fixating on countries or animals or whatever. We know that something is very wrong with Sarah. Something is clearly wrong with Tony too, some weird adoration complex, which he can only act out in reverse as the result of something unspeakable that happened to him in early childhood maybe? I actually don't care. But what I care about is that all this may have a detrimental impact on my own life in a profound way.

Where the fuck is this going you may be asking, and here is the answer: the *Financial Times* is the only paper left standing I can still read every morning without feeling ill. All the others, all purebreds once, have been crossed with tabloids, to prop up sagging circulations. Tabloid genes, unfortunately, are aggressively dominant in both the male and female lines. [Author's note: I think this sounds right, but please double check phraseology. Thanks.] The result is that every major national newspaper has gradually morphed into a tabloid, a trend reinforced by a collective loss of nerve and a sudden belief that all their readers are hapless morons with severe attention-deficit disorder who cannot focus on a single issue for more than ten seconds. Well, attention-deficit disorder never was my problem. [Editor: Nobody would ever accuse you of that.]

The *FT* has suffered wobbles too, but they are somewhat contained and efficiently channelled into their fortnightly *HOW TO SPEND IT* pull-out magazine, and that is fine with me. It is about lifestyle, fashion and interior design, and it peddles the kind of generic 'taste' that has become the hallmark of the international plutocracy: beige, bland, boring, pointless and ludicrously pricey. The purpose of all this is to allow the disposal of huge amounts of money, irrespective of merit.

Everything in the magazine is mind-blowingly expensive but the look can be easily achieved with little outlay at home: all you need to do is to take a double dose of Diazepam or whatever other tranquillizer you may have at hand. Talk to your physician first if you are unsure about the exact dosage. Place yourself in front of a mirror and slowly repeat:

'MONEY…MONEY…MONEY…MONEY…MONEY…
MONEY…MONEY…MONEY…MONEY…MONEY…
MONEY…MONEY…MONEY…MONEY…MONEY…
MONEY…MONEY…MONEY…MONEY…MONEY…
MONEY…MONEY…MONEY…MONEY…MONEY…
MONEY…MONEY…MONEY…MONEY…MONEY…'

You don't even need to mimic a robotic voice, it comes automatically.

To my mind *HOW TO SPEND IT* should really be called *HOW NOT TO SPEND IT*. Anyway, the magazine is easy enough to deal with: you pull it out and throw it away and keep the rest of the paper. Now to have Tony Blair defend himself on page 11 is as bad as having selections from *HOW TO SPEND IT* appear randomly across the main paper. It would turn the paper into something akin to the *Daily Telegraph*. The beauty of the *FT* is that it is one pitch all the way through, matter-of-fact, no nonsense, no frills, no gossip, no distraction, no waste of time. Having Tony Blair explain himself in the middle of all this would obviously endanger this tranquil and reliable state of affairs. And this is where it gets personal.

If the *FT* decided to merge the main paper and *HOW TO SPEND* or let people like Tony in on a regular basis I would lose the only paper I can still actually read without getting either outraged, frustrated, bored or ill pretty much instantaneously. So I have to fight back. I send the following email to letters.editor@ft.com:

> **Dear Sir**
>
> **Do you really believe that giving voluntary space to Tony Blair to explain yet again that he is not to blame for Iraq will do the integrity of your paper any good?**
>
> **If you cannot puzzle out the answer I am happy to come over and explain.**
>
> **Yours sincerely**
>
> █████████████

[Author: This email was actually sent to the *FT* at 8:07 am on 23 June 2014]

In reality I never write to editors, for two reasons. First, I believe that all letters to editors automatically go into the bin. Second, emails suffer the same fate: it is very possible that letters.editor@ft.com is set up in such an ingenious way that anything incoming is automatically redirected to 'junk'. It is much more effective to pick up the phone, call a friend who you know shares your opinion and have a really good, heartfelt, five-minute bitch.

This is when I call Sarah and she does not answer her phone.

Looking at the *FT* again later in the day I notice something amusing at the end of Tony's column:

**The writer was prime minister of
Britain from 1997 to 2007.**

I had nearly forgotten.

If the *Financial Times* journalists cannot see why it may be not such a hot idea to give Tony Blair space to vent his deranged ideas it might help clarify things if they started reading the *International New York Times*. On 26 June it carries the following headline:

Israel's Puppy, Tony Blair[*]

More locally even the *Daily Telegraph* gets it. Perfectly illustrating the level of hysterical self-righteousness that Tony Blair has reached – he can no longer open his mouth without something offensive coming out – it has the following story:

Blair: It's not about making money, I have less than £20m[**]

We all should agree: let's talk about Blair if we must, but let's not give him a platform to do the talking.

I order a second pot of tea:
    'Would you like this on a tray, sir?
'Yes please.'
We are getting there.

---

[*] Marwan Bishara, *International New York Times*, 26 June 2014, p. 7.
[**] Matthew Holehouse, *Daily Telegraph*, 22 July 2014, p. 10.

A little later a pageboy arrives with an envelope addressed to:

The Author
    Room 225-6
        Claridge's
           Brook Street
              W1K 4HR

Inside is a paperback copy of F Scott Fitzgerald's

The Diamond as Big as the Ritz

It bears a dedication as follows:

'For the Author –
I understand that you have finished the book and that
what is left to do is editing and typing. Well done.
    The grateful Proprietor'

[Author's note: I am touched. I never thought that he had any sense of humour.]

I have become aware of pageboys. They are cute, polite, snappy and efficient. I use them now all the time for any sort of errand. Andrea says I need to be careful not to run them ragged.

A pageboy arrives with a parcel. It contains a green blanket and a note:

'Dear ▇▇▇▇ **– as promised,**
    Angela'

Yuck. I thought she had taste. The green is a terrible shade.

I write a note:

> 'Dear Angela –
> Thank you so much for the green blanket – how could
> you have guessed that this is my favourite colour?
> It will become a very active protagonist in the novel,
> more like a performance prop.
> Many, many thanks.
>   XXX The Protagonist'

A second note reads as follows:

> 'Dear Doro –
> As promised, here is the Green Blanket – you deserve it.
> I have chosen the green especially, it goes with the colour
> of your eyes. You could use it like Linus in *Peanuts*
> whenever you have to deal with loons. There are plenty
> about. It takes one to tell them.
>   Lots of love, The Protagonist'

[Doro: You manipulative son of a bitch.]

I dispatch a pageboy with both notes and the blanket.

Returning to my suite from a little stroll down Bond Street
I notice the bathroom looks like it has been lightly sprayed with
a pale-brown liquid, like weak tea. Droplets are everywhere, on
the mirror, in the sink, the bathtub, all over the floor, the
window. I am a little taken aback: am I really that messy in the
morning – and is The Scar still oozing that badly? But then
I realise that the ceiling is actually dripping water. It's coming
down in steady drips – drip, drip, drip – through various gaps
between ceiling panels and the glass recess of the light fixture.
Oh my God, the upstairs bathroom is leaking! I am petrified:

Will management make me move out of the room? What would this mean for the novel? As author and protagonist will leave the room together the moment the novel is finished, making the author move to another room before he has done his job in effect means the end of the novel. It will have to be abandoned in mid-sentence and binned. I am petrified and in a state of acute anxiety. THIS CANNOT HAPPEN! NO, IT CAN'T.

I race downstairs to reception and ask for the duty manager. I explain to him that there is water coming off the ceiling in my bathroom, not a lot, and that I am not much worried about it, AS LONG AS I DO NOT HAVE TO MOVE ROOMS as I am in the midst of writing a novel about Room 225-6. I explain to him the author and protagonist conceit. Moving rooms would be a disaster, the END OF THE PROJECT. The great thing about inside Claridge's is that nobody ever judges you. Whatever you, the customer, say or request or DEMAND goes, no questions asked. The duty manager takes it all in calmly and tells me not to worry, he completely understands, he will send housekeeping and the in-house maintenance guy right away. He hands me his business card. If there is a problem can I please call him immediately. He apologizes for his surname. I read the card:

CLARIDGE'S*

ALEX DROWN
DUTY MANAGER

---

* In gold lettering, the rest in black

124

Shortly after I get back to my room a maid arrives. She is carrying an armful of freshly laundered, lightly scented, fluffy bath towels, each embroidered in gold thread with the Claridge's crest, which she dumps on the floor and then systematically spreads over every surface in the bathroom, floor, tub, sink, altogether about a dozen towels. A second maid follows with more bath towels, and she adds another layer to her colleague's handiwork. A little later the maintenance guy arrives. I let him into the suite and follow him to the bathroom. He looks at the ceiling and chuckles:

'Oh no, not again.'

'Yes, exactly like in the TV documentary.'

'Yup. Have you seen it?'

'Yes, only a few days ago, the concierge lent me the DVD.'

'Funny, isn't it?

'Very.'

Here is my chance, I think:

'May I let you in on a secret?'

'Sure.'

'I am here to write a novel, it is called "Room 225-6". It is about my recuperating from cancer.'

I motion at The Scar.

'I need to stay in this room, otherwise I will have to abandon the novel.'

I explain to him a bit more about the post-modern nature of the project, the author-and-protagonist conceit, The Political Prisoner in Room 212. He really gets it.

'Wow. How amazing. I can't wait to read the book.'

'Will you please work extra-hard on stopping the leak so that I can stay in the room?'

'Sure.'

I write down his details. His name is Neil, and he is on extension 7520. I am in safe hands; I can relax.

A little later a pageboy arrives with a black cardboard box. It contains a number of smaller wrapped items and a note:

> Dear ███████
>
> We were very glad to welcome you to Kallos Gallery last week. It was lovely to find a few moments to chat. We hope we can look forward to welcoming you again soon.
>
> Your recent ordeal sounds quite trying, and we are very sorry to hear of it, though glad to see you now well on the mend. My colleagues and I here at Kallos thought that you might appreciate a bit more looking after, if your good and caring friends and their generous Claridge's gift are falling short of expectations. Enclosed are a few little things to help fill, while away, sweeten, and generally enhance your period of convalescence – which we all hope will be swift and complete.
>
> Do please come visit us again while so close. Until then enjoy these small tokens, and all our warmest wishes for your good health, from your new friends at Kallos.

The note is signed by Alexandra, Liz, Beth, Glenn and John-Paul. I open the little packages. There is some loose Darjeeling tea, coffee, chocolates, and a DVD. I think, oh no, not another *Inside Claridge's* DVD. I open the package, and it is actually the rival documentary on the Savoy. I read somewhere that it is really boring, like a corporate promotional. Still, it's a good joke. The last package contains a puzzle, made up from a photograph of the Medusa Bowl. Mind-blowing.

Kostas arrives. He is a young Greek artist, a friend of Antonio's. He is here to research images of various aeroplane diagrams that I want to use in a presentation. I am after images of single-propeller planes (the kind Tintin would fly), as well as single and twin-jet planes. I won't go into detail about this because it is, as far as the narrative of this book is concerned, of no consequence. He is also here to help finalise preparations for this evening's party at my home, food shopping and setting up everything in the afternoon.

We are talking about this and that, about the papers, and about how Tony Blair obviously had managed to breach security at the *FT*, to get into the composition room and to sneak his self-justification piece in. We talk about the novel. I am still not over the shock of the leaking ceiling and what a narrow escape I had. I trust Neil, and I am sure he will sort out the leak as promised so that I do not have to move rooms. Still, there is a nagging fear – what if he can't fix it and I will have to move rooms after all? How will I be able to save the novel, because I obviously won't finish typing it out in twenty-four hours or so, unless I do an all-nighter that will definitely push me over the edge? There is also another problem: I have not yet collected enough material to flesh out the story sufficiently. Some of it I could obviously make up, still I feel that ending up in another room would definitely break the spell, and I may have to concede that I cannot finish the novel. There is fear in the air, and I am tense and unhappy. Kostas and I come up with some elaborate, mad constructs to compensate for eviction from 225-6. I could insist that the hotel moves me to 212 – at least I would then stay in the narrative continuum or whatever you want to call it, so the writing of the novel could carry on. Either I would have to share with The Political Prisoner (is he gay?) or he would have to move to another room. He is so unappetizing I would rather have nothing to do with him, so I guess he will have to move. None of this is particularly elegant, nor does it add momentum to the narrative. It is clunky, but it might have to do. All this keeps Kostas and me spinning along happily.

I learn much later that I nearly did poor Kostas's head in that day. I would not shut up and was batting ideas like nobody's business. He arrived home after the party in a state of utter exhaustion and with a roaring headache. He thought that there was definitely something seriously wrong with me. I was mental.

I absolutely hated the party at my home in Kentish Town. It was the usual crowd, 100-odd people, noisy, boisterous and drunk. A jolly good time was had by all except me. I felt excluded and marginalised, a stranger, like I had crashed this event, knew nobody and could not insert myself into any conversation, however hard I tried. I did not enjoy the food and I did not enjoy the drink. I was off everything. I felt truly depressed and very low. I learned later that I was actually working the room animatedly from one end to the other. I was, so it seemed, in top form, if not a little manic. By about ten I had enough. Mandana and I grabbed our dogs and went back into town on the C2 bus. We get off on Regent Street; she headed back to her flat in Soho and I returned to Claridge's. I felt exhausted and blue, ready for bed. I poured myself a glass of whisky and sat down. What a failure the whole evening had been, not just for me but for everybody, what a complete, utter, embarrassing failure, oh dear. In fact the party roared on until just before midnight when the champagne ran out, and the Ridinghouse gang finally had enough and turfed everybody out. I am about to drag myself to bed when there suddenly is a sharp rap. I open the door.

Doro told me much later what had happened at the party. A man whom she had never met before had introduced himself to her rather insistently. She did not catch his name. She thought he was creepy-looking, like he had spent too much time indoors, away from the sun. He was clutching a grubby and frayed Claridge's laundry bag. It was obvious that he knew nobody at the party and nobody knew him. He hovered round the buffet, pushed himself in line and piled his plate to the brim with foodstuff, wolfed it all down in a corner of the room, came

128

back for seconds, and the poor waiters could not refill his champagne glass fast enough. His table manners were execrable, and it was all a rather disgusting and sorry sight. Once he had finished eating he had engaged Doro in a convoluted conversation, she could not remember what he was on about – it was not very interesting. To be absolutely honest, she may have been too tipsy on champagne to follow the man's story. Hard as she tried she could not shake him off, he would not let go. He finally managed to sit her down at my desk in the study and came right to the point. He was here, he told her, to make her part of what without doubt would be the greatest publishing sensation since Aleksandr Solzhenitsyn won the Nobel Prize for Literature in 1970. He opened the grubby laundry bag and pulled out a tattered, stained, handwritten manuscript. This, he explained excitedly, was his diary. It documented his thirty years in a latter-day gulag, incarcerated at Claridge's, the prisoner of sinister political forces beyond his control. It was to his mind, the perfect illustration of the post-modern, late-capitalist condition, an innocent man pushed to the limits of human endurance by sloppy room service and surly hotel staff. The pageboys in particular would not let any chance pass to mock and humiliate him. Their cruelty knew no bounds.

He was here to give her an opportunity to make literary history. He and she would become household names. What was he, after all, but a Nelson Mandela figure for the twenty-first century? She looked at him stunned. Alcohol alone surely could not account for this. Was the man on drugs? She carefully signalled to one of the Ridinghouse juniors to come and rescue her, got up and handed the stranger her business card and suggested that maybe he give her a call at the office if he wanted to take things further.

He looked at her card: 'Why does it say "Ridinghouse"?'
'What do you mean?'

'Well, I thought this was a Random House party?'
Doro concluded that the man was definitely on drugs and
carefully explained. He looked at her in disbelief and fury,
grabbed his binder and bag and stormed out, nearly knocking
over a waiter balancing a drinks tray.

When I open the door the guy from 212 pushes his way in. He
is like a grenade with the pin already out, sweating profusely
and in a white rage. He is actually screaming at me. The Bitch is
growling too hard, and I am too exhausted and drunk to follow
what he is saying but I catch the occasional word:
> '…fraud…misrepresentation…money back…how dare
> you…'

On and on he rants. I pour him a drink to calm him down, not
easy when you are holding a snarling terrier by the collar at
the same time. The Bitch won't let go. I finally drag her to the
bedroom and shut her in. When I return to the sitting room
the stranger has calmed down a bit but is still very angry: I am
not Random House. He wants his money back. I am about to
tell him to fuck off when The Bitch starts clawing at the
bedroom door.
'Will you please excuse me for a moment?'
By the time I have managed to calm her down and return to the
sitting room the guy has gone. So has the bottle of whisky and,
as I only realise the next morning, the bowl of £2 coins from
the lobby. I drag myself to bed. What an arsehole, I think before
I fall asleep.

8

At about four I am awoken by the sound of cascading water. I stagger out of bed and turn the light on in the bathroom. The bathroom ceiling has started leaking again, this time it's serious, water is running like a waterfall. I wonder for a moment if Neil has anything to do with this. He obviously misunderstood me. I thought he would help with the plumbing, and I would drive the plot. Is he now driving the plot too? I call reception and report the leak:

'I am so sorry, sir. The night technician and maids will be with you right away.

'OK, thanks.'

Neil is of course not on duty, but instead a real dunce of a guy arrives. I always give people the benefit of the doubt and never, well, mostly never, judge by appearances. Here is the dialogue that ensues: He comes into the bathroom, looks around (I am in my sitting room, barely able to stand up with exhaustion), and after a few minutes joins me and starts talking.

'Looks like a flood upstairs.'

Wow, I am thinking, people have been given Nobel Prizes for much lesser insights. I am puzzled though: how can he be so sure?

He excuses himself and leaves the suite and a few minutes later comes back with an armful of bath towels, all freshly laundered. Here we go again, I think in amazement. He dumps the lot on the marble floor and kicks them in all directions, goes out, comes back with more, goes out again, comes back with even more. I would not be surprised if we will find a notice downstairs tomorrow saying:

WILL ALL GUESTS PLEASE
SHARE BATH TOWELS
BETWEEN ROOMS
(The General Manager)

because The Nobel Prize Winner has used up most of the supply for today in the bathroom of Room 225-6 in about five minutes.

After he has finished spreading towels all over the place he takes down two ceiling panels and takes a good, hard look.

He returns to the sitting room.

'Sir.'

'Yes?'

'It's coming from upstairs.'

He starts explaining to me, in monotonous voice, the ins and outs of Claridge's plumbing, all six floors and 257 suites and rooms, down to the smallest detail, the intersections of electricity and plumbing, how dangerous this can be, the intricacies of the heating system, the air-conditioning plant on the rooftop, recent major maintenance work, the old heating system versus the new one, its advantages and disadvantages. On and on he drones. He will not shut up. I finally have to disrupt him sharply and tell him that I am really not interested in the detail of all this. To be candid, I actually don't care. He looks stunned and a little hurt. Could he maybe spare me the nitty-gritty and just give a summary?

'Well sir, it is definitely coming from upstairs.'

'Really?'

'Yes.'

Jesus, I think.

Personally I feel that the guy is completely wasted here at

Claridge's. He should seek employment with NASA. With his intellect finding water on Mars will be a doddle.

A maid arrives with another armful of towels. They are now spread everywhere and spill out of the bathroom. I go back to bed but cannot sleep. I finally give up and get up. I am utterly exhausted and everything is hopeless. I am at my desk surveying the carnage, and then suddenly the screen goes blank:

9

When I come round I am alone, sitting at my desk, facing into the room. I don't think I have ever felt worse in my entire life. The room around me looks like it has died, like one of those slime-covered interiors in *Alien*, grey, dirty, trashed, and there are cobwebs everywhere. Everywhere. Towels are spilling out of the bathroom, and my personal belongings are strewn all over the sitting room. It looks like I have been burgled. Every surface is covered with manuscript notes for the novel; it looks like a crazy person has placed little reminders to himself everywhere. There is madness in the air, and fear, and confusion. How can I possibly stay in such a filthy place, I think to myself. How could I have been so deluded as to have chosen this dump of a hotel in the first place? I am alone. How will I ever get myself out of this mess? I call room service and order breakfast. 'Good morning.'

   'Good morning, sir.'

'Could I please have my usual, Darjeeling, toast and apricot jam.'

   'Of course, sir.'

'Thanks.'

   'Good-bye.'

Breakfast arrives. On a trolley. Never mind.

What can I do? How can I save myself? I cannot figure it out. Things are hopeless. At about seven o'clock I stagger back to bed but I cannot sleep. Thoughts are racing. My life is a mess, I am a failure, on every level, and I am sick. I am paralysed with fear. I will not survive this. On and on it grinds. I drift off, come round, start thinking, drift again, on and off and on and off.

My phone rings just after 8.30. It is Cordelia. Where was I? Was I OK? No, I am not OK; could she please come round and have breakfast with me? She knows me well enough to realise that something is seriously wrong and comes over right away.

I order her coffee and a croissant (delivered on a trolley) and we talk, or rather she listens to me ranting on about my screwed-up life and my anxieties. I am on a roll. She has to leave after an hour or so to see another Pilates student, and I am left on my own. The room looks unbelievably drab. The phone rings again. It is Great-Ormond-Street Richard. He is in Spain.

'Are you OK?'

I am so relieved to hear his voice.

'No, no, I am not OK; you must help me to get out of this. I am frightened. I do not know what to do.'

We are having a conversation, I am trying to explain, but I am aggressive and angry. He does not understand me. Nobody understands me. Everybody is so slow, but I am really fast and frightened of it.

He tells me to calm down.

'How?'

'Just stay there, don't move and I will organise help.'

'I need help now. I cannot wait,' I wail.

I am furious with him for not understanding, for not dealing with things that instant.

'Just wait.'

'No, don't go. I am frightened.' I am pleading. 'I need help now. I need to stop things from spinning; it is making me ill.'

'Just wait.'

'I need some medication to slow things down. Please.'

I am literally clinging to my chair, fearful that everything may speed up again. I really could not take another round of it.

Richard promises help, as soon as he can possibly organise it by phone, from Spain.

'Maybe I could take one of the Diazepam I have left for my needle phobia as a stop-gap?'

He thinks that might be an idea.

'OK, wait, I will go and get one of the pills.'

I go to the bathroom, take a pill and come back to the phone. Thank God I am very suggestible, and the pill to my mind takes immediate effect.

'Will you be OK for a bit?'

'Yes.'

'OK, just don't move, I'll call you back in a little.'

'Bye.'

'Whatever you do don't move. You have to promise.'

'I promise.'

'Bye.'

I am sitting on my chair and wait for the Diazepam to kick in for real.

The pill works very quickly, and I calm down. I know that I should not move, that I promised to stay put until help arrives. I ignore instructions and decide that I need to take charge, of the room, my life, the future. I am not mad, after all, I have concluded, and the best way of proving this to myself is to take control. I have a shower and get dressed and go downstairs to reception and speak to the manager.

Thank God Alex is on duty. I explain to him very briefly what has happened:

'I am afraid 225-6 is a bit of a mess, there was another leak from upstairs and I had a mental meltdown, so the room needs some attention.'

He is very sorry and promises to do whatever it takes to help. Could he maybe send five or so maids upstairs to clean up?

'Of course sir, I will send them right away.'

I go upstairs again and within a few minutes a fleet of maids arrives and start tidying up. They remove towels and trolleys and breakfast things and laundry, hoover the carpet, re-stack the mini-bar. I collect all the manuscript notes. I am fearful that just looking at them will make things spin again, so I stuff the lot into a Claridge's laundry bag which I bury in a drawer in the bedroom. Out of sight out of mind, I think.

One of the maids comes into the sitting room:

> 'I am sorry sir, I am trying to make the bed but the little dog won't get up.'

I follow her into the bedroom, and there is The Bitch curled up on the bed. She has slept through the whole drama of the last few hours. How typical, I think to myself, what a selfish little bitch. I pick her up and take her for a quick walk round the block. When I return to the room everything is tidy and glossy again.

The phone rings again. It is Sarah. It turns out that a whole support network has been put on red alert; Doro has spoken to Richard, Richard to Sarah, Sarah to Bridget. Everybody is concerned and everybody is ready to step in and help. Would I like her to visit? Yes please. She says that she will be with me in about an hour and rings off. A few minutes later the phone rings again. It is Richard. He tells me that they have found a psychiatrist who can see me at 7 that evening. He gives me the address. Harley Street. I can relax. Help is just round the corner.

Sarah arrives, and we decide that we should have a picnic in Green Park. We buy sandwiches and mineral water on the way over. There is a greengrocer at the entrance of Green Park and we get some cherries. The weather is glorious; we hire two deckchairs and enjoy the sunshine. I tell Sarah about the previous night and my fears. I am fine now, the Diazepam is definitely working. I tell her about my appointment with the psychiatrist later in the day. Sarah is very sympathetic; she sure understands madness. I am thinking it takes one to tell one but I am not saying anything. I watch Sarah from under my sunglasses. Would I like some cherries, she asks.

'Yes please.'

She then starts doing something very odd. She takes the cherries out of the brown paper bag and carefully spreads them on the lawn in front of her. She then sprinkles water on every single one from her mineral-water bottle. Her concentration is awesome.

'Sarah, what are you doing?'

'Washing the cherries.'

'But why?'

'Because they are really dirty. You can't be too careful.'

Oh dear, here we go again, so it's not just dog's anuses she has a problem with. Cherries too. Poor woman. I could take her to Harley Street in the evening, and the psychiatrist could talk to both of us; we could make it a sort of group therapy. On second thoughts, this is not such a hot idea.

Sarah and I wander back to the hotel, and she says good-bye. I take a nap. I wake up at about four. I can no longer tell the time because for some reason my watch stopped working. It just stopped. I decide to take The Bitch for a walk to Mappin & Webb in Regent Street. That's where I bought the watch, a Cartier Tank, only about three months ago.

We get to the shop.

'Good afternoon.'

'Good afternoon, sir, how may we help you?'

I take the watch off my wrist, dangle it in front of the guy and explain that I bought it here a few months ago and that it no longer works.

'Oh, I see, let me take you to the maintenance counter.'

He takes me to the basement, and I have to start all over again.

'How may I help you, sir?'

I dangle the watch and explain again.

'Do you have the Cartier guarantee card?'

'No, I don't.'

'I don't think we can help you without that.'

'Well, you'll have to.'

'Do you have a receipt?'

'No.'

'Oh there is really nothing we can do.'

'Really?'

'Yes. I am sorry, sir.'

She has obviously no idea how lucky she is that I am on Diazepam and that I am really trying to keep things calm.

I explain to her:

'Now there is a number on the back of the watch and that surely will match your records, and somewhere it will tell you when I bought this from you.'

'I am sorry, sir, without the receipt number and the guarantee card we cannot help. Cartier will not deal with this.'

I am now getting really annoyed, Diazepam or not.

'I actually do not care if Cartier will deal with this or not – that's your problem. I bought the watch from you, and I want you to sort this out for me.'

She gets funny again, 'Sir, I am afraid I cannot help you.'

I finally have enough. I look her straight in the eyes and lower my voice to a faint whisper:

'Now listen carefully. I have just been through major cancer surgery, and I have no energy to waste on a pointless conversation with you. I am here to ask you to fix the watch that you sold me three months ago. I don't give a damn about Cartier's guarantee. I am here under my rights, under the Consumer Protection Act, so please deal with this without any further delay. Have I made myself absolutely clear?'

I obviously have, because her tone changes instantly. It always works, I call it the cancer voodoo.

'Sir, why don't you sit over there whilst I sort this out for you.' She takes me to a sofa. 'May I offer you a drink?'

'Some water would be great.'

'Still or sparkling?'

'Still.'

'And would the little dog like some water too?'

'Uh, I think she is fine, thank you.'

She gets back behind her counter to call Cartier. They agree right away to have the watch sent to Paris overnight and repaired. The only problem is that now I am without a watch.

'Would you have another identical watch?'

She does not quite get what I am driving at so I have to explain. 'I want to buy a second, identical watch.'

She gives me a funny look but checks her computer anyway.

'Not here, sir, but there is another in one of our branches.

We could have it over here by tomorrow.'

'Great. Let's do this. Why don't you call me as soon as the watch arrives and I will come in and get it.'

All this is not as extravagant or impulsive as it sounds; I always buy two of everything I like, watches, items of clothing, sunglasses, it makes life so much easier, in case you have misplaced or lost one of the pair. I just had not got round to getting the second Cartier, but as I am in here anyway I might as well sort it out now. I also feel flush as I just had a refund to my credit card from the hospital.

Leaving Mappin & Webb I am still without a watch and that really drives me to distraction – I sleep with my watch on and never take it off. I feel naked and insecure without. I decide that I will go on to the Swatch shop on Oxford Street. What, I wonder, would a seriously crazy person wear watch-wise to see his psychiatrist? I chose a slightly oversized, bright red Swatch. Combined with the scar, the shirt-front and the fact that I wear my watch on my right wrist, it is perfect, the kind of look a talentless wardrobe intern would clamp on a minor actor with a walk-on part in a not particularly high-profile Hollywood movie. I hand the shop assistant the watch I have chosen and walk over to the till.

'I don't need the box, I'll just take the watch.'

The assistant looks at me: 'You need to take the guarantee card.'

'Oh, don't worry, I don't want that either.'

'You have to, in case something goes wrong.'

I explain that I have never in my life invoked a guarantee on a £30 watch. I don't mean this in a snobbish way.

'I really don't need the guarantee card.'

'I am afraid you have to take the card.'

She too has no idea how lucky she is that I am on medication. 'Well look, if it is so important and makes you happy why don't you fill in the card and throw it away on my behalf?'

She looks at me disapprovingly, and then she does exactly that: she takes the guarantee card out of the plastic watch case, fills it in with Biro, stamps it, staples the till receipt against it, puts the card back into the case and then throws everything theatrically into the waste bin under the counter. Wow, and I thought I was the crazy one here! I return The Bitch to the hotel and set off for the psychiatrist.

Turning into Harley Street I get a bit nervous. I mean I have never met the guy, and I have never in my entire life been to a psychiatrist before, and here I am with an awful lot to tell and explain. I have a friend who has gone for decades, twice a week, and she is still only at the beginning of explaining. I ring the doorbell and an assistant leads me into an all-oatmeal waiting room: oatmeal walls, oatmeal wall-to-wall carpet, oatmeal-oversized sofa. Not very exciting, I think, but then I remind myself that excitement is not what we are trying to achieve here, we are after the opposite. Oatmeal is a good start.

After a little while the psychiatrist comes to fetch me. He looks like a psychiatrist from central casting, dark blue suit, white shirt, black-rimmed glasses, slicked-back black hair. His consulting room is oatmeal too. The conversation is very businesslike. We get through the preliminaries fast.

'There are a number of general questions I have to ask you to begin with.'

'Like what?'

'Do you ever think about suicide or self-harming?'

'No.'

More follows, about any medication I may be on, any psychotic episodes I have suffered, routine.

The best question: 'Do you see secret coded messages on your TV screen?'

'I don't know.'

He sits up at that: 'Why are you saying this?'

'Because I don't have a TV.'

We get through the general stuff. I then set out why I am here and what has happened to me. He lets me talk and only cuts in occasionally to clarify.

I start off by describing the events of the last few weeks and last night. He interrupts right away:

'What exactly do you mean when you talk about dinner for 120 at home?'

'Exactly that: dinner for 120 at home.'

I decide not to mention that at the very moment I am sitting in his office I am hosting a dinner for 35 at Sartoria Restaurant for Alison Wilding to celebrate the unveiling of her sculpture, *Shimmy*, a work commissioned by the Crown Estate for one of its new buildings on Regent Street. The psychiatrist would find this too difficult to understand, and I need to keep him focused.

I talk about my life, the recent cancer drama and my recuperation stay at Claridge's and what I have been up to in the last two weeks or so, and after about thirty minutes he tells me that it is quite obvious what is happening to me, nothing a course of medication cannot sort out. I have heard this one before, still I make him write his diagnosis on the back of his business card:

Manic Psychosis
Chemical and Manic Defence

He hands me the card and explains. Much of what has happened to me since the operation is just pathology: the never-ending entertaining at the hotel, *Ulysses*, The Little Mondrian, the writing of the novel, it all points in the same direction, a manic-psychotic defence to overcome the surgical trauma I have suffered. Secretly I am rather proud of the diagnosis, surely the first case of self-inflicted manic psychosis ever, at least in part. I feel assured; at least I now know what is wrong with me. There is still some time left so the conversation turns more general, and we talk a little about the novel and how it will end, with the making of the movie based on the novel. The psychiatrist takes the whole thing in his stride and even playfully wonders who might take his part in the movie. Before I leave he hands me a prescription.

'Take half a pill in a morning and a whole in the evening.'
My last question concerns my living arrangements. What am I to do, move back home or stay at Claridge's? He looks at me earnestly.

'I know the place well. You have to get out of there sooner rather than later.'
He tells me that he will ring on Friday evening to find out how I am doing and assures me that everything will be fine.

I walk back to the hotel, hugely relieved, and have a pageboy fill my prescription. I have a light supper on my own and go to bed early. With the medication I sleep like a baby, right through until eight o'clock, for the first time in a fortnight.

Doro rings me the next morning to update me on the dinner for Alison. It was a huge success, though I was much missed.

There was a toast to me. I wish I had been there, but that really was not possible.

Thursday and Friday pass uneventfully. I take it easy. All social engagements in my diary have been cancelled, and I only have one or two friends over for lunch and dinner, no more tea parties, no more constant traffic. Oddly enough the Harley Street psychiatrist does not call on Friday evening. I am a bit taken aback by this, I mean if you can't trust your psychiatrist to ring when he says he will who can you trust? I am not too worried about this though and take it as a sign that he must think that I am OK and that the crisis has passed. I never hear from him again, though he sends in a colossal bill for the initial consultation, which makes me think that I am in the wrong business.

I take myself off the medication, and this has no discernible effect; things don't speed up around me, and my sleep pattern stays the same too. Saturday and Sunday are good days. I open the laundry bag with the manuscript to no averse effect, add a few notes and fill in missing bits in the novel's outline. I manage to sort all notes into an overall structure under six headers.

A number of things became clear: the whole great anxiety about the novel was complete nonsense. Whereas before I was fretting and driving poor Kostas and everybody else mad with my fear about having to leave the room or not before the novel is finished, now I think who cares? I have enough material, and what I am missing I will just make up. Another pre-crisis conceit bites the dust as well, the manic idea that everybody should be referred to by their first name only. It's the kind of idea that could overwhelm a novel easily and turn it into a bore, and get it singled out by an impatient critic for the harshest basting. The new me decides that you can either go by first names or not, it makes no difference, whatever sounds best in a particular place goes. As for the conceit of author and protagonist leaving the room in sync, well, it too is not that interesting – and if you really want to keep it up who is going to tell that they actually had not? The author sure won't, so nobody will ever know.

Before the crisis I had lost my ability to distinguish between fact and fiction. I was actually labouring under the delusion that I could drive reality like a fiction generator: I was in charge of reality. I was trying to spin as many plates as possible, the more the merrier, and was worn out by the sheer hard labour of having to keep a record of it all. Some of the notes in the bag make no sense whatever, I was in such haste. Others are crystal-clear:

The difference between life and
fiction is structure.

A particularly chilling one reads:

Micro-managing reality
DANGER

I should have followed my own advice.

Doro comes for tea. On the way up the lift guy asks her if she is here to visit the gentleman in Room 225-6.
    'Yes. Why?'
    'Is he your father?'
    Am I really looking that old, post-surgery?

The Bitch and I return to Mappin & Webb to collect the second watch.
    'Good afternoon, sir. How may I help you?'
I explain.
    'Do you have your order receipt?'
Is this some sort of Mappin & Webb in-house joke? Our

conversation goes nowhere and the woman in the end just walks away in frustration. She sends over another assistant, tiny, well-turned out, Chinese, perfect English with no accent whatever.

I explain to her again.

'Can we please make this easy, I want you to find the watch, take my credit card, process the payment, hand me the watch. I don't want a Cartier box, a faux-velvet pouch, a guarantee card, a Mappin & Webb VIP membership or whatever is going today, and I don't want gift-wrapping either. Do you think this will be possible?'

She looks at me matter-of-factly.

'Of course, sir.'

She proceeds accordingly and hands me the watch.

'I hope you don't mind my asking. Where are you from?'

'China, sir.'

'I'd love to go to China.'

'Where to?'

'Shanghai.'

'It's a very modern city, Shanghai.'

'I know. Which part of the country are you from?'

'Inner Mongolia, sir.'

I thank her and say good-bye. Why does it take a girl from Inner Mongolia to treat me like a human being in a luxury goods shop in central London, I wonder. The Bitch and I return to the hotel and take a nap.

Our last day but one, and the whole place works like clockwork.

'Good morning, sir.'

'Good morning.'

'How are you today?'

'Oh, much better, thank you.'

'I am so glad.'

Everybody is in the picture, we are greeted left, right and

centre, everybody cares, everybody is interested. Maybe a notice had appeared on the staff information board:

HANDLE WITH CARE
GUY IN 225-6 HAS GONE OVER THE EDGE
NOT DANGEROUS

The Bitch is doing her routine to the hilt, charges up the corridor like a banshee and saunters down the staircase like she owns the joint. This morning: about eight good-morning-sirs and three extensive conversations about The Bitch.

On the way down I pass Thomas, the general manager, on the staircase.
'Good morning.'
   'Good morning to you.'
If we were making a movie this would be a pitch-perfect single-take scene.

We join Mandana and Jezebel in the Park, and the two dogs carry on with the abandon of puppies. Mandana and I talk about Andrew, her boss and my landlord. He is not having a great time. He tried to play hero the other day by tripping a Soho burglar with his left (or right?) foot. What is it about 70-year old guys and macho pretensions? The burglar was duly apprehended, but Andrew ended up with a badly fractured foot that needed surgery, metal plates, screws, the works. It is not mending too well. To cheer him up I tell him that when he is out and about again I will take him to Clifton Nurseries to select a big terracotta pot and a tree for the little courtyard between the Ridinghouse offices and his restaurant.

7 am I have slept soundly and am woken up by the sound of cascading water in the bathroom. Here we go again, I think, this is getting really boring. I call reception and report the incident.

Five minutes later The Nobel Prize Winner arrives and I lead him into the bathroom. He looks at the ceiling.

'There is a problem', he says.

NO SHIT MAN I want to say, but I don't.

He beetles off and returns with the customary armful of white towels, which he spreads all over the floor. By now the flood has turned into a trickle. The Nobel Prize Winner stares at the ceiling again and then turns to me:

'There is definitely a problem.'

I am glad that we have established this.

The Floor Manageress comes in with two maids. She is extremely apologetic about this morning's leak. I tell her not to worry, I am perfectly fine about everything, find things hilarious actually, because all this is just further copy for the novel I am in the midst of writing. The bathroom incident provides perfect copy, especially when it occurs three times in a row. The manageress does not quite understand what I am on about, but the maids do and guffaw. I turn to one of them and say that I was thinking of renting Room 225-6 again when the book comes out for a small series of celebratory afternoon tea parties. Open laughter. She is a smart cookie. I tell her if the novel becomes a success I could be the first customer who came out of Claridge's richer than he went in. She roars and her boss gives her a very disapproving look.

Two more maids arrive with armfuls of bath towels; the laundry room must be working overtime. They dump them in front of the bathroom, and I steal three. I mean there is so much stuff flying about, surely nobody is keeping track of numbers?

Breakfast.

'Good morning. Could I please have a tray with a pot of Darjeeling, white toast, very lightly done, and apricot jam?'

'Very well sir. Darjeeling, toast and a selection of jam.'

'No. Darjeeling, toast and APRICOT JAM.'
'Would you like some pickle too?'
'Sorry?'
'Some pickle?'
'No. No, definitely not. DARJEELING, WHITE TOAST AND APRICOT JAM.'
'OK, OK, very well.'
'Thank you.'
Could this be The Nobel Prize Winner's brother I am dealing with? Or is having won a Nobel Prize a precondition for working at Claridge's? I have to remember to ask one of the maids about this the next time we have a chat.

I decide to take tomorrow (Sunday) off.
[Editor: Who do you think you are? God?]
[Protagonist: LOL]
[Writer: LOL]
[Doro: Guys. Cut it out.]

No bathroom leak this morning. Am I relieved or disappointed? Neither.
I am toying with the idea of calling in The Nobel Prize Winner anyway: where do you think the water is not coming from today? Not from above or not from below? Nice idea but a little too obvious. I mean anyone with an ounce of imagination could write up the ensuing dialogue, so why bother?

During our morning walk though Green Park Mandana and I touch on many diverse subjects. Had I read about Tracey in last night's *Evening Standard*? I detest the *Evening Standard*, it is sloppy and boring, and no wonder they have to give it away for free.
'No. What's she now on about?'
'She was talking about her fear that *Bed*, which Charles was

about to sell at Christie's, would be lost for the nation, would probably end up with some Chinese or Russian collector right in the middle of nowhere. This could make her life hell because she would obviously have to go again and again to supervise installation and de-installation. Was she not already busy enough?'

I swallow hard. Mandana continues:

'She regrets that she had not made the work fifty years ago, because then it would fall under the Waverley criteria, have its export delayed so that a national museum could start a fundraising drive and rescue it for a grateful nation.'

'Are you pulling my leg?'

'No.'

I think, wow, this is delusional right off the scale, but I suspect that Mandana is indeed pulling my leg. People have started planting bits of conversation with me to secure their place in the novel. Unfortunately whenever I am really in a hurry The Bitch goes double-slow, but we finally make it back to the hotel. I head up to my room and Google. It's all there, and here is the link: http://www.standard.co.uk/news/london/tracey-emin-i-cant-make-my-bed-stay-in-uk-but-no-gallery-here-can-afford-it-9567764.html. Some things you just couldn't make up.

Thankfully we all can relax about *Bed*. It turns out that a German count was the buyer, and he has since lent it long-term to Tate Modern. You could not make this up either.

Monday. Doro and I take a late afternoon stroll in the neighbourhood. I ask her to go to Victoria's Secret with me. It is about five o'clock, so things have calmed down a little and there is no longer a queue outside the shop. We walk right in. Marble and faux gilding everywhere, of a vulgarity that makes your average Las Vegas hotel lobby look like Mies's Barcelona Pavilion. THIS PLACE IS AMAZING! The shop is absolutely rammed with teen girls, mostly in hot pants, and Middle

Eastern matrons in full black, and one or two single guys. The guys look furtive. I wonder what are they doing in here, are they cross-dressers shopping for gear? They must be. The merchandise is stunning; I mean you can BUY THREE PAIRS OF FRILLY KNICKERS FOR £27! This may be part of the summer sale, I can't remember, and they are obviously not 100% silk. The stuff is out of this world, and the word 'gaudy' does not do things any justice. I suggest to Doro that we buy a pair of pink, glittering panties for everyone at the office, guys and girls alike, but she wants nothing to do with this plan. I really hate it when her American Puritanism gets in the way of things. There is a perfume bar with about fifty-odd different Victoria's Secret scents, with names like DREAM ANGELS or LOVE IS HEAVENLY or EAU SO SEXY or NEW! PINK WILD PINK or VICTORIA'S SECRET BOMBSHELL FOREVER or whatever. They all smell identical, like bubble gum. I am completely in love with it all. I could have discovered Victoria's Secret years ago but refused to go in because of some misplaced snobbery. Well, we all make mistakes. The place is all about sex but only as a thought, not for real. Sex is the elephant in Victoria's room, so to speak. The best way to keep your fantasies in check is to come in here and have them lived out for you as graphically as possible. It's clean and cheap, and it is easy to get to – there are about a thousand branches all across America and the company is in the midst of an aggressive international expansion drive. Victoria's Secret is reassuring because we all know of course what happens when the line between sex fantasy and sex reality is crossed. When the line between fantasy and reality is crossed, we only need to remember poor Kevin Spacey in *American Beauty*: you get your brains blown out by the suppressed-gay father of your daughter's dope-dealing boyfriend, that's what happens. After about ten minutes Doro and I leave the shop and return to Claridge's.

Since then I have registered my email address with

Victoria's Secret, and I now receive daily updates. Today's message read:

Here's what to wear this fall

Two days later:

Psst, your next bra is 20% off!

Four days later:

Final Hours!
PANTY PARTY
7/ $26.50

Seven for $26.50! Still, after another week I unsubscribe.

The Bitch and I are at the Indian summer stage of our stay, and she is at her most playful.

Our last day but one. This morning The Bitch peed on the white fluffy mat in front of the bathtub, a perfect yellow bullseye surrounded by white. It's the kind of joke The Bitch finds funny. [Editor: Me too.]
[Doro: She can be so naughty.]
[Editor and Doro: LOL.]
I use the hair dryer and dry the mat and hide it in the present cupboard. I will have it framed behind glass and hang it in one of the guest bedrooms in Norfolk.

Word is out that we are about to quit the hotel. One of the maids strikes up a conversation:
    'So you are leaving tomorrow?'
'Yes, I am.'
    'Sir, we are all very sad about this.'

I smile at her.

'Me too. But all good things have to come to an end.'

'I understand that you are writing a book about us.'

She seems a little nervous about this.

'Yes, I am. But don't worry, it will be very affectionate about all of you.'

She pauses for a moment and then continues:

'Writing a book is really interesting because it helps others. If they do not understand a situation like Claridge's your book might help them to do so.'

I am stunned.

I ask for her name: 'Katalin, sir.'

'Where are you from?'

'Hungary, sir.'

'How long have you been working here?'

'About two years.'

'Do you enjoy it?'

'Yes, very much, sir. This is one of my favourite rooms.'

'Why is that?'

She looks round the sitting room.

'Because I have looked after some very famous guests in here.'

'Like who?

'Oh, I could not say, sir. That would be indiscreet.'

I explain to her the first name or redaction spiel that runs through the novel.

'You need not tell me any names, we just put in a redaction and then it looks as if you told me but you had not.'

She is delighted with this.

'What about your own name or would you rather have ▆▆▆▆▆▆ or a generic name, like "The Little Hungarian Maid"?'

'Oh, I would be very pleased to read my own name.'

We are parting fast friends.

I am having a little chat with Alex, the duty manager. He is concerned, is everything OK and am I enjoying the rest of my stay? Yes, absolutely. He is worried of course that the three leaks and Black Wednesday might somehow overshadow my stay, and, God forbid, will find their way into the novel. Is there anything they can do for me? There is really nothing amiss and my stay has been a smashing success but there is actually something I would like. I really could do with some Claridge's bath towels, and I don't want to steal them.

'Well, now you are asking – do you think it would be possible to let me have a dozen big, fluffy, embroidered hotel bath towels, by way of compensation for the three bathroom leaks? I mean it has been a strain.'

I give him my best long-suffering look.

    'I don't see why not, yes of course.'

'Wonderful. Could you have them sent up to my room please.'

He hesitates:

    'Well, I will have to order them and that will take a few

    days. You see, we are currently low on towels.'

I look at him:

'Are you? Well, I am not surprised as maintenance seem to use them to mop up spillages.'

    'Yes but they use the used ones.'

'No, they don't. They always use freshly laundered ones, and in unbelievable quantities.'

    'They don't, do they?'

'They do.'

    'Really?'

'Yes. Every time.'

    'Oh dear.'

    This morning I am feeling deeply sentimental in the happiest way imaginable. I order breakfast:

    'Good morning, sir.'

'Good morning to you.'

    'Your usual?

'Yes please.'

'Darjeeling, white toast and apricot jam.'
'Exactly.'
   'On a tray?'
'Yes please.'
   'Very well, sir.'
'Good-bye.'
   'Good-bye.'
It's all finally working like clockwork, just when I am about to
check out.

Half an hour later I order a second pot of tea.
 'Good morning. Could I please have a second pot of Darjeeling.'
   'Of course, sir.'
It arrives on a trolley. Never mind, in my present frame of mind
I think this charming.

Last night in my suite. Dinner with Maureen. Loyal friend,
always fun. Tomorrow I will go home.

On our last morning The Bitch and I head for Green Park. It is
another sunny, glorious morning. On the west side of Berkeley
Square we pass a bum in a doorway. I gently wake him up and
give him a £20 note. I am not sure if he is the same bum I gave
£20 the previous morning. All bums look the same, like bums.
'Excuse me, did I give you £20 yesterday?'
   'No.' He nods to the next doorway. 'You gave it to him.'
I hand him another £20: 'Could you please hand this to your
neighbour when he gets here?' On second thought I add: 'Or
you may decide to keep the money for yourself.'
   I do not want to pose him with a moral dilemma he might
not be able to resolve. I mean if I had nothing and a stranger
hands me extra money for a fellow bum who isn't there, how
would I feel about passing it on? Quite frankly I would keep it
for myself, wouldn't you?

The bum looks at me and gives me the biggest grin I ever had from a bum. We understand each other. I am only glad that he has no idea what I have been up to the previous three weeks round the corner in Brook Street. If he had he would probably crumple up the notes and throw them in my face, and who can blame him? The Bitch and I carry on towards Green Park. When we get to the other side of the Square and into Fitzmaurice Place there is another bum in a doorway. He is barricaded behind a wall of cardboard boxes, and there is a strong smell of fermenting piss. I wake him gently and give him £20. Now I need to find a cash machine.

Why am I telling you all this? I have recently been struggling through Thomas Piketty's *Capital in the Twenty-First Century*, and I want to save you the effort. It's not that Piketty is unreadable, quite the opposite, what he says is set out clearly and without jargon, and even a layman can follow the argument easily, but it is a long book and the above is a convenient shorthand illustration of the insight at the centre it.

What Piketty is concerned about is the growing gulf between a tiny elite to whom an ever-increasing proportion of wealth accrues, and the rest of us who have to do with less and less. This trend began about thirty years ago with Reaganomics and the Thatcher revolution. It has taken hold all over the world, and with the collapse of the Soviet Union a quarter of a century ago it is now the only show in town. At the centre of it stands a mantra that says that excessive wealth for a very few is good for everybody, because that privileged wealth in the end benefits everybody. It trickles down in all sort of permutations: as investments (creating jobs), spending on goods and services, taxes, charity. It sounds good in theory. There is only one problem with this: in reality it is not true. We have reached a point where those who are the richest preach trickle-down hardest but refuse to practise it at all, so of course it does not work. But what is even worse is that everybody else, even the victims of all this, have been brainwashed into preaching the mantra too. So now we are at that surreal stage where our politicians, Conservative and Labour alike, fall over each other to vilify the poor and underprivileged, make their lives even more miserable by coming up with ever more punitive and petty measures, like the bedroom tax, for example. All this happens without anyone raising an eyebrow. Not even the Church protests much. There is of course method behind this: if you blame people for their own fate you render them invisible. That is exactly what is what has happened to the poor, the chronically ill, the mad, the uneducated, they are blamed for their own fate and conveniently forgotten. If, on the other hand, you suggest that taxes on the wealthy should possibly rise just a smidgen, or you propose something as mildly sensible as maybe, just maybe, making real-estate taxes a tad more progressive, you will be shouted down and called all kinds of unpleasant names, as if you are suggesting turning the UK into the North Korea of Europe. We have reached a very sorry state of affairs, and it will take some doing to get out of it. Personally I think if we all began giving money to bums that would make a good start.

Another delivery, a bottle of Japanese Bourbon with a note:

> **'Dear Author**
> **I hear the book is nearly done.**
> **Congratulations.**
> **I can't wait to read it.**
>   **Best,** ▬▬▬▬▬▬▬

I hate Bourbon. Into the wardrobe it goes.

Another dream: All rooms in the hotel are inhabited by authors feverishly working on novels about their stay at Claridge's. There are 257 writers at it, all at the brink of nervous breakdowns. Those novels that are deemed finished are surreptitiously taken away by maids. Authors whose work is considered beyond hope are put on medication by a team of five in-house psychiatrists and encouraged to leave the hotel as soon as possible. All this has to do with a secret takeover of the KGB station by Random House five years ago. All the KGB guys are now in the pay of Random House, and matters have much improved in the basement: you now hear jokes and banter. Random House of course does not need hundreds of novels about writers stuck in Claridge's, but that is not the point. The near-identical manuscripts are carefully edited to fit whatever genres are needed. Apparently changing an 'Inside-Claridge's' novel into a political memoir is the easiest transformation to perform. This explains the strange tone of Tony Blair's autobiography.

Classic FM 7 o'clock news: Dolly Parton drew by far the largest crowd of any performer at Glastonbury on Sunday evening. Asked by a reporter why she wore all white she explains that she wanted to be visible to the people right at the back. She also thought that white went well with mud. What a star.

Packing up all my stuff and emptying the present cupboard takes two hotel maids over two hours. To begin with there is a misunderstanding: they suggest taking a series of Polaroid photographs of the suite with all my things in situ, the books, The Little Mondrian, the Picasso portrait of Cecchetti, the ushabtis, the Landy Cézanne, the content of my wardrobe, the present cupboard. My stuff is then carefully wrapped in silk paper and stored in clear plastic crates. This is so that on my next visit everything will be forensically put in place again in my room, as if I had never left. Apparently that is what regulars do with their belongings. It takes a bit of explaining that this is not what is needed, though I am tempted to go along with their suggestion. This is, after all, the perfect excuse, if a pathetic one, to come back: all my stuff is still here. I could come back once a month for a few days. What a stupid idea! Sometimes I really wonder about myself. Once we have cleared up the misunderstanding the maids set to work, and we end up with two trolleys full of luggage and cardboard boxes. (It will take me four days to unpack at home.) The booze arsenal is something to behold. I count thirty-nine bottles of Japanese whisky; at the rate I am going this will last for about ten years. I set aside duplicate presents to pass on. One is a copy of *An Exuberant Catalogue of Dreams*, a book about Americans who arrived in England since the late nineteenth century and made the country-house idea their own. I will give it to Paul, an American expat, anglophile, and my Norfolk landlord since 1999:

> **'Dear Paul –**
> **This is one of the many presents received during my recuperation at Claridge's. I have a copy of the book already so this is a duplicate.**
> **Who would be more suitable but you to pass this on to? Another American Dreamer. Thank you for having me in the stable block.**
> **Much love, The Protagonist'**

I am having my morning call to find out if Sarah had a good night and not too many disturbing dreams about small and large dogs with personal hygiene problems. She sounds cheerful enough and rattles on about what she had been up to the previous evening. Our conversation turns to general topics when the hotel's fire alarm goes off. It is a high-pitched, continuous shrill beep, unnerving but not unnerving enough to disrupt the conversation. We carry on regardless but after about five minutes Sarah says that maybe this is serious, I should grab The Bitch and The Little Mondrian and head for the lobby, just in case. We say good-bye, and I take The Bitch but leave The Little Mondrian behind – I mean I don't want to look like a complete Charlie when we get to the lobby. The Bitch is racing up the corridor like the place is really on fire, down the staircase and onto the ground floor. There is not much activity in the lobby, not a sea of guests in their pyjamas and robes ready to evacuate. Rich people obviously don't rescue themselves, they wait to be rescued. Actually nobody much cares. I was right not to bring The Little Mondrian. I head for the concierge's desk. Miles is on duty.

'Good morning, Miles.'

    'Good morning, sir.'

'What's going on?'

    'I am sorry, sir, it's the fire alarm. We cannot find the switch.'

Really? I am puzzled. Is Miles related to The Nobel Prize Winner too?

    It takes them another fifteen minutes to turn the alarm off.

10

Two years later.

The movie rights for *Room 225-6* had finally been bought by an adventurous Hollywood production company, Moving-On Films (M-OF), owned by Brad and Angelina. The deal did not earn the Oracle Cancer Trust quite as much as hoped for, but as the chief executive said, ▇ K is still ▇ K. The poison defence was expertly de-activated by the promise of an obscene fee to Kevin.

A team of the best scriptwriters was employed to turn the book into a script. The team struggled. A second team was retained, soon augmented by some clever UK kids and the fellow who had written 'Daneton Abbey'.* Various how-to-move-forward meetings had been convened in Los Angeles, San Francisco and New York. The book was by and large considered crap by everybody who had anything to do with the project. But we all know how it is with big-budget scenarios, after a certain way in nobody will call it quits and abort. Everybody is just too busy extracting large sums of money for themselves, so everything carries on to the bitter end, regardless.

At one of the final big script conferences (this time held at one of the bungalows at the Hotel Bel-Air) Brad attended and had pretty much the casting vote. As no consensus could be reached by those present he made all the important decisions: It was agreed that the dialogue would no longer mimic The

* [Author: This is another private joke.]
[Editor: Obviously.]

Bitch's walk – whatever that meant anyway – but was to be modelled closely on *The Wolf of Wall Street*. London would become Manhattan, the Marsden Sloan Kettering and Claridge's the Carlyle. Easy.

As for the protagonist, the character was deemed completely incomprehensible. Instead a specially convened focus group recommended rewriting the part from scratch and modelling it loosely on Larry, the most powerful contemporary art dealer in the world. The Bitch morphed into a Great Dane called Hamlet. The Little Mondrian was replaced with a six-foot Andy Warhol Dollar Sign painting. Britney agreed after long negotiations to play herself in three thirty-five-second cameos, for which she was paid ▬▬▬▬▬ in advance and ▬▬ % of gate. When Kevin heard about this he went into a sulk and sent his agent in. He too managed to get himself quite a bit more.

They may of course have got the wrong Britney: nobody was able to say for sure which Britney had actually stayed at Claridge's. We will never know for sure. Claridge's does not reveal customer details, and the real Britney does not say either. She very quickly had figured out that ambiguity on this point worked to her advantage. The studio was determined to get the real one. So by some weird fluke it is possible that the Japanese Britney is played by the real one in a movie after a novel partly informed by a fly-on-the-wall TV documentary. This, I guess, is what they mean when they are talking about reality biting fiction on the arse.

Filming started before the script was finished but things ran into trouble pretty much immediately. Both Sloan Kettering and the Carlyle refused to co-operate 'on principle'. This turned out to be a matter of money, as always. Two teams of lawyers huddled for six weeks and tried to thrash out a compromise, but to no avail. The money demanded was just too stupid. The Royal Brompton Hospital and Claridge's both waded in opportunistically and said that they would be willing to get on board for less – and they even accepted the temporary name changes: in the movie the actual London hotel was renamed Carlyle, down to the lettering on the façade. During filming this caused some arriving guest acute discomfort; they thought they had gone out of their minds. The Royal Brompton Hospital likewise had its nameplates changed to Sloan Kettering. At least three patients missed important medical appointments because they could not find their hospital. Two of the patients and the estate of the third settled for substantial six-figure sums with the production company. The exact amount cannot be revealed because of the terms of a confidentiality agreement signed by all parties.

The entire film crew was transferred from New York to London to make a movie set in Manhattan. The team took up three full floors at the Carlyle (aka Claridge's). Preparations for filming of what was to be one of the movie's key scene began right away. The management of Claridge's was accommodating and efficient as always. Detailed planning of the installation and de-installation of the jacuzzi started immediately. The director thought that it might be a good idea to remove one of the bathroom walls as well to get more room for crew and cameras. Structural engineers were called in. Their advice was unequivocal, a steel beam would have to be inserted to keep the entire building sound. Six days were allowed for the steel beam, and a further four days for the jacuzzi (as before). The insertion of the steel beam necessitated the evacuation of two floors of paying hotel guests and the cancellation of two tea sittings in the lobby and four lunch and dinner sittings in the restaurant, 'just to be on the safe side'. All of this of course was charged to M-OF. Work began soon enough and finished on time (but not on budget). When the director saw the rushes he deemed the lighting inappropriate, and the art director on second thought felt that the tiling looked 'too old-fashioned and a little dowdy'.

The entire bathroom was retiled in the palest grey Carrara marble (two days, overnight, and well over budget) and the scene re-staged (four days, on budget). A third retake was ordered and approved by the studio (four days and well, well over budget). When the bills for all this arrived at the M-OF finance office the man in charge was found sobbing uncontrollably at his desk. He has since been on indefinite sick-leave. Before the jacuzzi was taken down again, the standby script team decided that it would be fun to add a scene with Britney actually using the jacuzzi.

Britney said 'no'.

The whole Britney aspect of the novel led to a huge fight with Legal at Ridinghouse. Legal wanted her name redacted or even, if possible, the whole scene left out, as they thought it was potentially libellous. As the protagonist I like to disagree, on the grounds that a) this is fiction and even Britney and her lawyers might get the point, and b) I am actually doing her a huge favour by sending a subliminal message that could, if she were to read the novel carefully, change her life dramatically for the better. Because what I am thinking here is:

'No, Britney. Absolutely not.'

This is, after all, what she has been hoping for all her life, and what she is replying, as if by osmosis, is:

'Jacuzzis make me puke.'

To my mind this marks amazing progress. I agree, it is only a start, but somebody had to make it, and I did.
[Editor: The Harley Street psychiatrist was wrong. He thought you were a loon. You are actually off the chart.]

174

Legal kept on fretting. Britney's lawyers might take umbrage at her appearing, against her own will really, in a novel. There was actually a legal precedent here: Apparently Scarlett Johansson had sued a French novelist for embroidering his fiction with her name. This was even reported in the *Financial Times*, as an aside in an article by Gaspard Koenig under the headline:

Sarkozy's noisy return will drown out voices of progress*

Scarlett had actually won the case and had been awarded Euro 2,500 in damages by a Paris court. It was not exactly a resounding victory as she had asked for Euro 50,000 in damages and an undertaking that the book would not be translated into other languages or turned into a movie. The *Guardian* carried a story about all this, with detailed information.** The paper quoted the French author, Grégoire Delacourt: had he known Johansson would kick up such a fuss, he said, he would have chosen someone else as his icon of modern-day beauty.'
I thought she might send flowers as [the book] was a declaration of love for her, but she didn't understand it at all,' he said. 'It's a strange paradox – but a very American one.' Just another cheap shot at Americans, Doro muttered. In any event, I think Legal can relax, and here is why: if the real Britney sues we just say that we are talking about the other one, if the Japanese sues we say that we mean the real one. If both sue – well I hope we'll have a bright judge with a sense of humour:
    'Will the real Britney please stand up – case dismissed.'
If I was Britney's lawyer I would not go after Ridinghouse – there is no money there, so why bother? The Japanese doppelgänger, on the other hand, looks really very, very rich. [Author: I cannot wait for my bunch of flowers from Britney.]

* *Financial Times*, 5 July 2014, p. 11.
** *Guardian*, 4 July 2014.

I am sorry to say that the new Britney did not last even twenty-four hours. By next morning lawyers acting on behalf of her agent got in touch with the M-OF legal department. Britney after all, it transpired, was willing to overcome her aversion to jacuzzis, provided that she was rewarded appropriately. Her agents and lawyers had done a quick back-of-an-envelope calculation: to their estimate the crew on standby in London ready to film cost about $1.2m per day. Three floors of the hotel, the cast, crew, back-up, technical, catering – it all added up quickly. There were trucks full of lights, wardrobe and make-up, parked on both sides of Brook Street from one end to the other. Westminster City Council was earning a packet too, just on parking permits.

The M-OF guys were on tenterhooks and ready to sign up to anything: they needed not make a back-of-an-envelope calculation, they had the actual figures. The daily outlay for just waiting and doing nothing was $1.447m. Every day, like clockwork. Finance was getting very antsy.

> 'So after all Britney is willing to do the jacuzzi scene, provided she is properly remunerated.'

'Wonderful. What sort of figure do you guys have in mind?'

> 'Well, actually we were hoping you would make us a starting offer.'

'I think you should go first.'

> 'Uh. We can wait. Why don't you call us when you are ready?'

'No. No, wait. Please.'

> 'Yes?'

'What about $2m up front?'

> 'Make it $3m and you got a deal.'

'Uh, I need to speak to Finance first.'

> 'Oh come on. You don't.'

'All right then.'

> 'Plus all legal fees.'

'This is so greedy!'

   'And your point is?'

'OK, let's go with it. Done.'

They shake hands.

   'Great. We'll have the paperwork with you in an hour
and you can wire the funds before close of business
this afternoon.'

Except they didn't, because they had missed the day's wire
deadline by a few minutes.

Filming finally resumed twenty-four hours later. There was a
further half-day delay because Britney was not happy with
her trailer. In the end she settled for a suite at the hotel instead.
They got her Room 225-6, perfectly nice and comfortable,
but by her standards it was an insult, a mere dank hole in
the wall. On arrival she reduced two maids to tears, just for the
heck of it.

Filming got off to a bad start. Not even for $3m was Britney
able to disguise the fact that jacuzzis were no longer really her
gig. Up to her neck in bubbling, steaming foam and coated in
make-up – nothing could hide that she looked as if she had just
puked in the corner of her mouth. She was not a happy camper.
On the seventeenth retake things were getting ugly. Britney's
skin felt shrivelled up and itchy, her hair was a mess, and the
bath foam or whatever they put into the water made her eyes
stream. There was mascara running everywhere. She had a
roaring headache. The director too was at the end of his tether.
He and the art director finally decided to call it a day. They
would have the animation people photoshop a lovely, relaxed
smile on Britney's face, making her look like she enjoys jacuzzis
more than sex. The Britney-in-the-Jacuzzi scene was to take up
fourteen seconds in the final movie, probably the most
expensive fourteen seconds in film history. You blink and will

have missed it. Most people missed it because they were so bored with the film that they were asleep through most of it.

Even before the filming with Britney ended the creative team was beginning to have doubts that there was enough in the script to carry a full-length movie. The director too thought that something should be added. An emergency script-review meeting was convened in Los Angeles. Various ideas were bandied about. How about a romantic interlude between Kevin and Britney? How about turning this into a comedy about mistaken identities: could the Japanese Britney not be brought on board and play opposite the real Britney, with various men endlessly ending up in the wrong suites? What about a hot orgy scene, Britney, her doppelgänger, Kevin, Baron Thyssen (possibly played by Brad himself, wouldn't that be exciting?), the two butlers, and Thomas, Claridge's photogenic general manager, going at it hammer and tongs in the Royal Suite? You could rename the film *Room 22-69*, geddit? How about *Room 225-6* with a lesbian leaning, the two Britneys in the jacuzzi, steamy girl-on-girl action? A call was put through to Sam Taylor-Johnson, who had just finished her highly acclaimed *Fifty Shades of Grey* trilogy. Might she be interested in coming on board as a consultant? She, unfortunately, was not keen at all and felt that she had 'done sex' and was looking for something intellectually more challenging. Would M-OF like to have first crack at a script she was currently working on, an in-depth biopic about Victoria and David Beckham? A call to the manager of the Japanese Britney ended equally fruitless. She barely spoke English, it turned out, and she would only be available if she could bring her entire entourage, first class by Air Japan, personal assistants, secretaries, dressers, assistant dressers, make-up artists, two hairdressers, her two personal yoga teachers and three chefs (Japanese, French and vegetarian), as well as her security detail, altogether about thirty-five people, all of them to stay at Claridge's, preferably on one floor. Fortunately this was not possible at such short notice as the hotel was fully booked.

The M-OF finance department finally put an end to all this speculation. They insisted that no additional costs would be incurred and that the film would be finished as per original plan and budget.

After the jacuzzi fiasco filming of the scenes in the hotel's entrance lobby was scheduled. The hotel management had decided that days of filming in the lobby was just too disruptive. M-OF pleaded hard and offered obscene financial incentives but to no avail. Anticipating this, a plan B had been set in motion. Over the previous six weeks the entire lobby of Claridge's had been painstakingly rebuilt at Pinewood Studios. No expenses were spared. Everything was there, the fireplace (in working order), the crystal chandeliers, the portrait of Mrs Claridge, the furniture, the flower arrangements, the checkerboard floor, made from marble especially flown in from Italy and expertly laid by a team of twelve Florentine master craftsmen. Two hundred extras played milling guests and exhausted shoppers taking afternoon tea. Wardrobe had a field day. If you were led blindfolded onto the set you really could not have told the difference between original and copy.

The key scene was Kevin and Hamlet sauntering down the staircase as if they owned the joint. It wasn't clear what exactly the director had in mind, maybe some man-and-dog version of Fred Astaire and Ginger Rogers dancing, light as air? It quickly became obvious that Hamlet was great-looking, but he sure wasn't well trained. Truth be told he was dumb. It proved impossible to get him down the staircase in step with Kevin. The dog was easily distracted and wandered off in mid-take, or refused to move at all. The dog's trainer failed to get any commands across and was sacked. A dog whisperer was found in Hampstead but she couldn't get Hamlet to behave either. So the dog was put on a lead, and Kevin dragged him down the stairs – that, in any event, was the plan. The dog did not budge and growled at Kevin. They tried bribes: they put treats in the pocket of Kevin's suit, and the dog got completely overexcited. There was slobber everywhere. By early afternoon wardrobe had finally run out of replacement jackets for Kevin. Filming was called off for the day.

Word was out that *Room 225-6* was turning into a dangerous disaster for M-OF and threatening the credibility of those involved. There were dark rumours about angry backers and that the studio might not survive independently. The *Los Angeles Times* carried a long inside story about it all, revealing many embarrassing details. There was a *New Yorker* diary feature.* *Vanity Fair* too got in on the act:

ROOM WITHOUT SERVICE:
HOW BRAD'S M-OF HIT THE SKIDS**

It was one of those classic *Vanity Fair* suck-up jobs, you know, highly critical about 'the Hollywood system' yet still completely gaga about the stars. Brad even appeared on the cover of the magazine, looking happy and relaxed and sun-kissed.

A day later filming resumed. The dog handlers had decided to put Hamlet on doggie tranquillizers so that he was less excited and more manageable. A veterinary team was on standby. The vets gave Hamlet a dosage carefully calibrated to his body weight, but nobody had predicted how susceptible the poor beast was to his medication. Hamlet could barely stand up and

* *New Yorker*, 14–21 July 2017, p. 34.
** *Vanity Fair*, August 2017, pp. 67–74.

drooled like crazy. When he walked his knees buckled. He looked as if he was made of rubber. They tried the scene again, several times, to no avail. The dog rolled and stumbled like he was stoned. Twice he actually fell asleep in mid-take. Kevin was furious. On the fifteenth take the dog let himself be dragged down the staircase but suddenly stopped cold. Kevin yanked the lead and Hamlet tipped forward in slow motion and crashed to the ground without even a whimper. Kevin had just enough time to jump out of the way. Health and Safety immediately stepped in and closed the set. The director was ready to walk off the job for good but didn't because he really needed the money for his impending divorce.

The creative team finally suggested to drop the staircase scene and have Kevin and the dog come out of the elevator instead. For cost reasons it was decided not to rebuild the elevator at Pinewood but to film in the lobby of Claridge's, overnight so not to inconvenience hotel guests during the day. It took three days for Hamlet to sufficiently sober up. They set up cameras and lights in the hotel lobby at midnight and filming commenced at 2 in the morning. Two hundred extras were milling excitedly. They were all on double pay because of the time of day. They put Kevin and Hamlet into the lift on the third floor (entirely taken up by the film crew anyway).

'And…action!'

The elevator came down. Hamlet's owner had forgotten to mention that his dog suffered from severe motion sickness. The result was catastrophic. When the elevators door opened Hamlet bolted out as if possessed. The entire interior, the panelling, mirrors, the dinky gilt Louis-whatever wall clock, the lift-man's uniform, the little bench and Kevin's suit were covered in dog sick, and the stench was unbearable. There is a lot of vomit in a Great Dane. Filming was abandoned immediately. 'Out of order' signs went up on each floor and the lift cage was expertly steam cleaned in the basement, all charges to M-OF.

Kevin decided to take a break from filming. He had had enough of it all, but he also wanted to get a truer sense of what the character he was playing was really like and 'flesh out the part', so he asked his friend Larry if he could observe him for a bit and talk to him to get a sense of what being a big-shot art dealer was really like.

They had agreed that Kevin would come to Los Angeles, attend a Howard Hodgkin private view at Larry's gallery and a small dinner for the artist at Mr Chow's, and that Kevin and Larry would lunch together the next day and talk about Kevin's part in *Room 225-6*.

When Kevin got to the gallery the private view was already in full swing. The exhibition consisted of twelve small paintings, raw and emotional yet exquisitely beautiful. The show had been expertly installed over 20,000 square feet of space, each picture floating in a sea of concrete polished so high that every week at least two visitors suffered a gallery version of white-out, and ended up hugging the floor, moaning and babbling, and had to be helped off the shiny expanse by attentive gallery staff who took them by the arm and led them to safety. The private view was a huge success; the crowd was peppered with famous faces, there was Joan, Jack, Bruce, Nicole, Warren, Diane, Steve, Cate, Ben, Tom, Julia, Leo, Clint, Meryl, on and on it went, a sea of stars. They all were friends the way famous people in Hollywood are.

Dinner was a more intimate affair, sixty-odd people, and Kevin found himself seated next to Scarlett. This was not a coincidence, her publicist had called the gallery in the morning and insisted that she would be seated next to Kevin, otherwise she would not show. Scarlett knew Kevin vaguely and needed his advice. A week before her French agent had called and told her about an intriguing offer: was she prepared to take the part of herself in the movie after the novel she only two years ago had unsuccessfully tried to stop? The money on offer was out of this world. Still, she was in two minds. Kevin was in the midst of a similar experience, playing himself in a movie of a novel, so his take would be useful. She had heard the ugly rumours and of course had read the *Vanity Fair* article. She could not quite remember the name of the novel, was it *Room 212*? Something like it. Why the Manhattan area code, she wondered. How silly. Anyway, she was here to hear it from the horse's mouth.

After a bit of chitchat she came right to the point. How was he getting on with his hotel film? Kevin dropped his guard and launched into it like he was on a psychiatrist's couch. What a stupid mistake it all had been, how much he detested the vacuity of the book, its narcissistic self-involvement, its arty conceit! He had met the author, what an arsehole. He, Kevin, should have known from the start that playing himself playing Larry was just one twist too many. Instead he should have signed up for another three seasons playing a Washington monster. He told her all about Britney and Hamlet and the whole goddamned set-up at Claridge's, and explained the reason why he was in Los Angeles, to have lunch with Larry tomorrow to flesh out the character he was playing. To tell the truth, he was here to get away from London. He was sure the stupid film would bomb and be forgotten in five minutes. Yes, the fee he had been paid was ludicrous, it would give him complete freedom in the future to take on only projects he really wanted to do, irrespective of pay. Still, he felt ashamed about it all. It was one gigantic, unrelenting nightmare of his own making.

Scarlett told him about her invitation to play herself in a movie after a novel. She did not mention the French court case.

'Based on your own experience, what would you advise me to do? Should I or should I not take the part?'

Kevin turned to her and looked her deep in the eyes: 'Don't.'

There was a pause, and she excused herself for a cigarette and left the table.

She doesn't actually smoke. She went to the car park and called her French agent:

'Francois? Hi, it's me…Scarlett…yes, I know it is early, sorry…well, never mind…I have been thinking about the movie…yes, the one where I play myself…yes, the one we went to court over…no, I think people forget these things in no time…well, I have decided to do it, if they offer me 5… no, not euros, dollars…yes, dollars…and for an extra 2 I am happy to do full frontal and sex…yes, I am quite sure…yes anything, honestly…yes, even that…do you think you can swing this for me? Really? Well that would be great, good luck…yes…lovely, wonderful…yes…see you next week…bye.'

In the morning she got a text message from her agent:

'Congratulations all settled for 5 plus 2 filming starts in three months xxx F'

Scarlett was very happy.

The next day lunch was scheduled for 12.30 at the Hotel Bel-Air. For the occasion M-OF had rented one of the bungalows in the hotel's grounds, away from the pool area, which was such a hotbed of Hollywood gossip. Kevin had arrived early and was sitting at the table that had been set up on the terrace in front of the French windows. Waiters in white jackets were hovering. Larry was already forty minutes late.

Larry's empire was at its most expansive and powerful yet. He now had outposts in every time zone around the globe, twenty-four galleries, each doing ten exhibitions a year. In addition he attended thirty-three art fairs. In order to gain time

184

and stay in touch with everything Larry had taken to circling the globe in his private jet in eastward direction only. His work pattern, developed for him by an international management consultancy, was gruelling: He slept for half an hour and then attended to business for half an hour, slept again, dealt, slept again, dealt, and on and on. This way he was able to speak with each of his gallery directors at least once a day. Every second day he attended a private view and dinner at one of his outposts. He had overcome jetlag by making it permanent. Still the life he was leading was utterly exhausting, and he was beginning to wonder if it was really worth the effort.

Larry had had a morning from hell. Actually, every morning for him was a morning from hell. There was a problem at the Nairobi gallery; he couldn't remember what it was, the useless director had failed with something or the other yet again, but more worryingly the latest round of Western sanctions against Putin were biting in Moscow. Larry was unable to get any art in and any cash out. The staff was just sitting there, twiddling their thumbs and idly reading *Pravda* and Russian *Vogue*. In addition there were complications with his gallery catalogues: Suzanne, his publications director, had told him this morning that she finally had run out of art historians or critics to write essays, so she was battling an acute shortage of copy. They had tried everything, larger typeface, bigger margins, reprints. They couldn't make it work. There were about 250 catalogues each year, all centrally coordinated, lavishly produced with no expense spared and shipped to clients all over the world, an operation so vast that it required its own warehouse in New Jersey with a permanent staff of 25. The latest ruse to overcome this problem had been to invite topical non-art writers and pair artists with global celebrities for interviews. It had all gone spectacularly wrong with the Howard Hodgkin catalogue. The gallery had asked Thomas Piketty to write an essay. It opened with the words 'I don't know anything about art …,' and no amount of editing could render what followed any more meaningful. The publication director had solved the dilemma by printing the text in French only, hoping that none of the recipients spoke the language. The interview between Howard and Anna Wintour wasn't exactly a success either: the return of fur was not a subject Howard had much to say about. He couldn't care less, actually.

Larry was pissed off with everything, and to cap it all he now had to have lunch with Kevin, who was whiney about that stupid film he had got himself involved in. Larry could not even remember the title, *Suite something-something*? What, Larry wondered, could he actually tell Kevin about himself and his life as the most powerful art dealer on the planet? Not the truth, that was for sure.

His driver finally made it through the Los Angeles traffic, and Larry arrived at the hotel an hour and a half late. They said hello distractedly and sat down. The waiters took orders. Larry ordered steak tartare and Kevin a green salad with dressing on the side. They shared a bottle of sparkling mineral water. They started talking.

The conversation was deeply disappointing. Kevin was distracted and so was Larry. Neither was paying any attention to what they were saying or what they were listening to. Here is a complete transcript of their conversation, showing you, word for word, what each heard. Legal insisted that three names were redacted:

Larry: Blab bla blab bla bla bla blab bla blab la blab bla blab bla bla bla bla bla bla bla blab la blab bla bla blab bla bla bla blab bla blab la blab bla bla bla blab bla bla bla blab bla blab la blab bla blab bla blab bla bla bla blab bla bla la blab bla bla bla blab bla bla bla blab bla blab la blab bla bla blab bla bla bla bla bla blab la blab bla blab bla blab bla bla bla blab bla blab bla bla blab bla.

Kevin: Blab bla blab bla bla bla blab bla blab la blab bla blab bla blab bla bla bla blab bla blab la blab bla bla blab bla bla bla blab bla blab la blab bla Bblab bla blab bla bla bla blab bla blab la blab bla blab bla blab ▇▇▇▇▇▇▇▇ bla bla bla blab bla blab la blab bla blab bla blab bla bla bla blab bla blab la blab bla bla blab bla bla bla blab bla blab la blab bla bblab bla blab bla bla.

Larry: Blab bla blab bla bla bla blab bla blab la blab bla blab bla blab bla bla bla blab bla blab la blab bla bla blab bla bla bla blab bla blab la blab bla Bblab bla blab bla bla bla blab bla blab la blab bla blab bla blab bla bla bla blab bla blab la blab bla blab bla a bla blab bla blab la blab bla.

Kevin: Bla bla blab bla bla bla blab bla blab la blab bla blab bla blab bla bla bla blab bla blab la blab bla bla blab bla bla bla blab bla blab la blab bla Bblab bla blab bla bla bla blab bla blab la blab bla blab bla blab bla bla bla blab bla blab la blab bla blab bla blab bla bla bla blab bla blab la blab bla bla blab bla bla bla blab bla blab la blab bla bblab bla blab bla bla bla blab bla.

Larry: Bla bla blab bla bla bla blab bla blab la blab bla blab bla blab bla bla bla blab bla blab la blab bla bla blab bla bla bla blab bla blab la blab bla bla bla blab bla bla bla blab bla blab la blab bla blab bla blab bla bla bla blab ▇▇▇▇▇▇▇ bla bla la blab bla blab bla blab bla bla bla blab bla blab la blab bla bla blab bla bla bla blab bla blab la blab bla blab bla blab bla bla bla blab bla blab la bla bla.

Kevin: Bla bla blab bla bla bla blab bla blab la blab bla blab bla blab bla bla bla blab bla blab la blab bla bla blab bla bla bla blab bla blab la blab bla blab la blab bla bla bla blab bla bla bla blab bla blab la blab bla blab bla blab bla bla bla blab bla blab la blab bla blab bla blab bla bla bla blab bla bla blab bla blab la blab bla blab bla blab bla bla bla blab bla.

Larry: Blab bla blab bla bla bla blab bla blab la blab bla blab bla blab bla bla bla blab bla blab la blab bla bla blab bla bla bla blab bla blab la blab bla bla bla blab bla bla bla blab bla blab la blab bla blab bla blab bla blab bla bla bla blab bla blab la blab bla blab bla blab bla bla bla blab bla blab la blab bla bla blab bla bla bla blab bla blab la blab bla bblab bla blab bla bla bla blab bla blab la blab bla.

Kevin: Bla bla blab bla bla bla blab bla blab la blab bla blab bla blab bla bla bla blab bla blab la blab bla bla blab bla bla bla blab bla blab la blab bla bla bla blab bla bla bla blab bla blab la blab bla blab bla blab.

Larry: Bla.

Kevin: Bla bla.

Larry: Blab bla blab bla bla bla blab bla blab la blab bla blab bla bla bla bla bla bla blab la blab bla bla blab bla bla bla blab bla blab la blab bla bla bla blab bla bla bla blab bla blab la blab bla blab bla blab bla bla bla blab bla bla la blab bla bla bla blab bla bla bla blab bla blab la blab bla bla blab bla bla bla bla blab la blab bla blab bla blab bla bla bla blab bla blab bla blab bla.

Kevin: Bla blab la bla blabla.

Larry: Bla?

Kevin: Blab bla blab bla bla bla blab bla blab la blab bla blab bla blab bla bla bla blab bla blab la blab bla bla blab bla bla bla blab bla blab la blab bla Bblab bla blab bla bla bla blab bla blab la blab bla blab bla blab bla bla bla blab bla blab la blab bla blab bla blab bla bla bla blab bla blab la blab bla bla blab bla bla bla

188

blab bla blab la blab bla bblab bla blab bla bla bla blab bla blab la blab bla blab bla blab bla bla bla blab bla.

Larry: Blab bla blab bla bla bla blab bla blab la blab bla blab bla blab bla bla bla blab bla blab la blab bla bla blab bla bla bla blab bla blab la blab bla Bblab bla blab bla bla bla blab bla blab la blab bla blab bla blab bla bla bla blab bla blab la blab bla blab.

Kevin: Bla bla blab bla bla bla blab bla blab la blab bla blab bla blab bla bla bla blab bla blab la blab bla bla blab bla bla bla blab bla blab la blab bla Bblab bla blab bla bla bla blab bla blab la blab bla blab bla blab bla bla bla blab bla blab la blab bla blab bla bla bla blab bla blab la blab bla bla blab bla bla bla blab bla blab la blab bla bblab bla blab bla bla bla blab bla.

Larry: Bla.

Kevin: Bla blab bla blab la blab bla blab bla blab bla bla bla blab bla bla la blab bla blab bla blab bla bla bla blab bla blab la blab bla bla blab bla bla bla.

Larry: Bla?

Kevin: ▬▬▬▬▬▬.

Larry: Bla bla blab bla bla bla blab bla blab la blab bla blab bla blab bla bla bla blab bla blab la blab bla bla blab bla bla bla blab bla blab la blab bla bla bla blab bla bla bla blab bla blab la blab bla blab bla bla bla blab bla bla la blab bla blab bla blab bla bla bla blab bla blab la blab bla bla blab bla bla bla blab bla blab la bla bla.

Kevin: Bla bla blab bla bla bla blab bla blab la blab bla blab bla blab bla bla bla blab bla blab la blab bla bla blab bla bla bla blab

bla blab la blab bla bla bla blab bla bla bla blab bla blab la blab
bla blab bla blab bla bla bla blab bla blab la blab bla blab bla
blab bla bla bla blab bla.

Larry: Bla bla blab bla bla bla blab bla blab la blab bla blab bla
blab bla bla bla blab bla blab la blab bla bla blab bla bla bla blab
bla blab la blab bla bla bla blab bla bla bla blab bla blab la blab
bla blab bla blab bla bla bla blab bla bla la blab bla blab bla blab
bla bla bla blab bla blab la blab bla bla blab bla bla bla blab bla
blab la blab bla blab bla blab bla bla bla.

[Editorial: The actual transcript of this went on for twenty-six
pages. We cut twenty-three. We believe the reader gets an
idea anyway.]

Three months later the rough cut of the film was shown to Brad
and his creative team in Los Angeles. At the end there was
deadly silence. It was clear to all present that this project was
beyond help. Nothing, no amount of editing, fine-tuning,
tweaking, media spin, full-page advertising, absolutely nothing
would rescue this pup. Not even good old-fashioned bribing of
critics would do. It was agreed to finish the film and launch it
as inconspicuously as possible, say in the fringe programme of
the Danske Film Festival in Skive which runs exactly two days
before the Oscar ceremony. That should bury it.

When the finished movie finally was shown to a test audience,
composed of AB1-s, young, hip and intelligent, the result was
not encouraging: there was stony silence at most of the scripted
jokes and a lot of mirthless hilarity at all kinds of unexpected
moments. By the time the lights came up about half the
audience had already left. The film went straight to DVD. You
can save yourself the pain of watching it if you go on YouTube:
some poor soul with too much time on his hands has compiled

THE BEST MOMENTS OF *ROOM 225-6* (http://www.youtube
.com/watch?v=pNx3_qJUCC0). It runs for the whole of thirty-
seven seconds, fourteen of which are Britney in her tub. There is
also a mildly amusing puppet spoof. Personally I think at just
under a minute it is far too long (http://www.youtube.com/
watch?v=Tx1XIm6q4r4), though the glove-puppet Britney has
gained her own cult following. The movie did not make it on to
any of the WORST FILMS OF THE YEAR lists. We were talking
complete failure here, whichever way you looked at it. Anyway,
all this was yet far in the future.

11

Kevin returned from Los Angeles to London none the wiser. To his mind the lunch with Larry had been a complete waste of time. In the morning he went to his office at the Old Vic – he was no longer artistic director but he had retained a base at the theatre. Basil, his assistant, was a sweet 19-year-old whose father had bought him the three-months stint as an intern at an Old Vic fundraiser. To be absolutely honest the kid was not particularly bright, but he was also completely overwhelmed by Kevin's star power. Every time Kevin addressed him, Basil ended up in a terrible muddle. This morning he returned to his desk remembering something about sending some money to some German dealer guy in London for some charity or other. So the kid went on Google.

The next morning Angela sat in her office at the David Zwirner Gallery in Grafton Street, W1. For her life she could not figure out why Kevin was sending David a cheque for £500 'for charity'.

First night home. I am so happy to be back in Kentish Town.

I wake up in the morning and think WHAT A SCARY FUCKING NIGHTMARE I JUST HAD.

(June–September 2014)

Bibliography and filmography

Esther Addley, 'Assange's suitcase is packed, but is he going anywhere?', *Guardian*, 19 August 2014

Wes Anderson, *The Grand Budapest Hotel*, Faber & Faber, London, 2014

Cory Arcangel, *Working On My Novel*, Penguin Books, London, 2014

Clive Aslet, *An Exuberant Catalogue of Dreams: The Americans Who Revived the Country House in Britain*, Aurum Press, London, 2014

Brooke Astor, *Footprints: An Autobiography*, Weidenfeld and Nicolson, London, 1980

—, *Patchwork Child,* Weidenfeld and Nicolson, London, 1963

Esmahan Aykol, *Hotel Bosphorus*, Bitter Lemon Press, London, 2011

Fred Basten and Raymond Sarlot, *Life at the Marmont: The Inside Story of Hollywood's Legendary Hotel of the Stars – Chateau Marmont,* Penguin Books, London, 1987

James Scott Bell, *Plot & Structure,* Cincinnati, Writer's Digest Books, 2004

Arnold Bennett, *The Grand Babylon Hotel,* 1902; repr., Penguin Books, London, 1938

_, *Imperial Palace,* Cassell, London, 1930

Claude Berne (dir.), *Hôtel du Paradis,* Abordage Films, 2014 (film)

Frei Betto, *Hotel Brasil: The Mystery of Severed Heads,* Bitter Lemon Press, London, 2014

Anne Billson, 'What Scarlett Did Next', *Sunday Telegraph Seven Magazine*, 24 August 2014

Kevin Birmingham, *The Most Dangerous Book: The Battle for James Joyce's Ulysses,* Penguin Press, New York, 2014

Tony Blair, *A Journey,* Arrow Books, London, 2010

Carel Blotkamp, *Mondrian: The Art of Destruction,* Reaktion Books, London, 1994

Kathryn Bonella, *Hotel K: The Shocking Inside Story of Bali's Most Notorious Jail,* Quercus, London, 2012

Elizabeth Bowen, *The Hotel*, Vintage, London, 2003

Matthew Brace, *Hotel Heaven: Confessions of a Luxury Hotel Addict*, Random House, London, 2008

Taffy Brodesser-Akner, 'Can Las Vegas Save Britney? (and Vice Versa)', *Observer Magazine*, 13 July 2014

Charlotte Brontë, *Stancliffe's Hotel,* Penguin Books, London, 2003

Anita Brookner, *Hotel du Lac*, Penguin Books, London, 1993

Martine Buchet, *The Taste of Provence: La Colombe d'Or at Saint Paul de Vence*, Assouline, New York, 1993

Ron Carlson, *The Hotel Eden,* Norton, New York, 1997

Agatha Christie, *At Bertram's Hotel,* Harper, London, 1965

Anthony Cipriano (dir.), *Bates Motel,* American Genre Film Archive, 2013 (film)

Gordon Claridge and Caroline Davis, *Personality and Psychological Disorders,* Hodder Education, London, 2003

Laura Claridge, *Tamara de Lempicka: A Life of Deco and Decadence,* Bloomsbury Publishing, London, 2000

Isabel Clarke, *Psychosis and Spirituality,* Whurr Publishers, London and Philadelphia, 2003

Ronald Cohn and Jesse Russell, *Ayumi Hamasaki,* Books on Demand, Miami, 2012

Wilkie Collins, *The Haunted Hotel,* Penguin Books, London, 2008

Lance Comfort (dir.), *Hotel Reserve,* RKO Radio Pictures, 1944 (film)

Caroline Cooper and Lucy Whittington, *Hotel Success Handbook,* MX Publishing, London, 2010

Victoria Coren Mitchell, 'My Very Own Fifty Shades of Blue', *Observer,* 24 August 2014

Steve Dobson, *Unusual Hotels of the World,* Jonglez Publishing, Versailles, 2013

Philip Dodd, *The Reverend Guppy's Aquarium,* Random House, London, 2007

Adrian Edmondson (dir.), *Guest House Paradiso,* Universal Pictures, 2000 (film)

Imogen Edward-Jones, *Hotel Babylon,* Corgi Books, London, 2005

Ezra Elia and Miriam Elia, *We Go to the Gallery,* Dung Beetle Ltd, London, 2014

Mike Figgis (dir.), *Hotel,* Prism Leisure, 2001 (film)

F. Scott Fitzgerald, *Tender Is the Night,* Wordsworth Classics, London, 2011

James Ford, *Hotel on the Corner of Bitter and Sweet*, Allison and Busby, London, 2013

Giles Foster (dir.), *Hotel du Lac,* 2 Entertain Video, 1986 (film)

Nick Foulkes, *The Carlyle,* Assouline, New York, 2007

Thor Freudenthal (dir.), *Hotel for Dogs,* Dreamworks, 2009 (film)

John Kenneth Galbraith, *The Affluent Society*, Hamish Hamilton, London, 1958

Terry George (dir.), *Hotel Rwanda,* Lion Gate, 2004 (film)

Klara Glowczewska, *Condé Nast Traveler: Room With a View*, Assouline, New York, 2010

Meryl Gordon, *Mrs. Astor Regrets: The Hidden Betrayals of a Family Beyond Reproach,* Houghton Mifflin Harcourt, Boston, 2008

Edmund Goulding (dir.), *Grand Hotel,* Metro-Goldwyn-Mayer, 1932 (film)

Patrick J. Gullane, Paul Q. Montgomery and Peter H. Rhys-Evans, *Principles and Practice of Head and Neck Surgery and Oncology*, CRC Press, Boca Raton, 2009

Ed Hamilton, *Legends of the Chelsea Hotel,* Da Capo Press, Cambridge, 2007

Jessica Hausner (dir.), *Hotel,* Artificial Eye, 2010 (film)

Christopher Hears, *Britney Spears: Little Girl Lost,* Transit Publishing, Montreal, 2010

Patricia Highsmith, *The Two Faces of January*, William Heinemann, London, 1964

Victor Hirtzler, *The Hotel St. Francis Cook Book,* The Hotel Monthly Press, Chicago, 1919

Alfred Hitchcock (dir.), *Psycho*, Shamleigh Productions, 1960 (film)

R. W. Holder, *How Not to Say What You Mean: A Dictionary of Euphemisms*, Oxford University Press, Oxford, 1995

Osca Humphreys (dir.), *Inside Rolls Royce*, Channel Four, 2014 (television documentary)

John Irving, *The Hotel New Hampshire,* Black Swan, London, 2010

Peter Joehnk and Corinna Kretchmar-Joehnk, *101 Hotel Lobbies, Bars & Restaurants*, Braun, Salenstein, 2014

Eric Jorgensen, *Stern Drive: Service Repair Handbook,* Clymer Publications, Los Angeles, 1977

James Joyce, *Ulysses,* Shakespeare and Company, Paris, 1922

Frances Kiernan, *The Last Mrs. Astor: A New York Story*, WW Norton & Company, New York and London, 2007

Stanley Kubrick (dir.), *The Shining,* Warner Bros, 1980 (film)

Vivian Kubrick (dir.), *Making the Shining*, Eagle Films, 1980 (film)

Martin Nicholas Kunz, *Luxury Hotels: Best of Europe Volume 2*, TeNeues, Kempen, 2012

Enda M. Larkin, *How to Run a Great Hotel: Everything You Need to Achieve Excellence in the Hotel Industry,* How To Books, Oxford, 2009

Bruce Laughton, *The Euston Road School: A Study In Objective Painting,* Scolar Press, London, 1986

David Leavitt, *The Two Hotel Francforts,* Bloomsbury Publishing, London, 2013

Gemma Levine, *Claridge's: Within the Image,* Harper Collins, London, 2004

Mark Lloyd, *How to Buy and Run Your Own Hotel,* How To Books, Oxford, 2008

David Lynch (dir.), *Hotel Room,* Asymmetrical Productions, 1993 (film)

John Madden (dir.), *The Best Exotic Marigold Hotel,* Fox Searchlight Pictures, 2014 (film)

Francisca Mattéoli, *Adventure: Hotel Stories,* Assouline, New York, 2005

—, *American Hotel Stories,* Assouline, New York, 2009

—, *Escape Hotel Stories: Retreat and Refuge in Nature,* Assouline, New York, 2012

—, *The Luxury Collection: Hotel Stories,* Assouline, New York, 2013

Tilar Mazzeo, *The Hotel on Place Vendôme,* Harper Collins, New York, 2014

Mandy Merck and Chris Townsend, *The Art of Tracey Emin,* Thames & Hudson, London, 2002

Joseph A. Michelli, *The New Gold Standard: 5 Leadership Principles for Creating a Legendary Customer Experience Courtesy of The Ritz-Carlton Hotel Company,* McGraw Hill, New York, 2008

Howard Mittelmark and Sarah Newman, *How Not to Write a Novel,* Penguin Books, London, 2009

Deborah Moggach, *Heartbreak Hotel*, Vintage, London, 2012

—, *The Best Exotic Marigold Hotel*, Vintage, London, 2013

Franceso Monacorda and Michael White, *Mondrian and His Studios / Colour in Space*, Tate Publishing, London, 2014

Paul Moorhouse, Richard Shiff and Robert Kudielka, *Bridget Riley: The Stripe Paintings 1961–2014*, David Zwirner Books, New York and London, 2014

John Llewellyn Moxey (dir.), *Horror Hotel: The Gateway to Hell*, Waterfall, 1960 (film)

Charles Nemes (dir.), *Hôtel Normandy*, Studio Canal, 2013 (film)

Veronica Newson, *Ultraluxe Hotels: The Experience Awaits…*, John Wiley & Sons, Chichester, 2009

Chris Nineham, *The People Versus Tony Blair: Politics, the Media and the Anti-War Movement*, Zero Books, Ropley, 2013

Yoko Ogawa, *Hotel Iris*, Vintage, London, 2011

April Peveteaux, *Gluten Is My Bitch*, Tabori and Chang Stewart Inc., New York, 2013

Thomas Piketty, *Capital in the Twenty-First Century*, Harvard University Press, Cambridge and London, 2014

R. T. Raichev, *The Curious Incident at Claridge's*, Soho Press, New York, 2010

Arthur S. Reber and Emily S. Reber, *The Penguin Dictionary of Psychology* (third edition), Penguin Books, London, 2001

Alrick Riley (dir.), *Hotel Babylon*, 2entertain, 2006 (television)

Joseph Roth, *Hotel Savoy*, Hesperus Press, London, 2013

Alastair Sawday, *Dog-Friendly Breaks in Britain*, Alastair Sawday Publishing, Bristol, 2014

Karsten Schubert, *The Curator's Egg: the Evolution of the Museum Concept from the French Revolution to the Present Day*, Ridinghouse, London, 2002 (2nd edition)

Danielle Steel, *Hotel Vendôme*, Transworld, London, 2012

Polly Stenham, *Hotel*, Faber & Faber, London, 2014

Karen Swan, *Christmas at Claridge's*, Pan Macmillan, London, 2013

Genndy Tartakovsky (dir.), *Hotel Transylvania*, Sony Pictures Home Entertainment, 2012 (film)

D. M. Thomas, *The White Hotel*, Gollancz, London, 1981

Bill Tikos, *The World's Coolest Hotel Rooms*, Collins Design, New York, 2008

Sherill Tippins, *Inside the Dream Place: The Life and times of New York's Legendary Chelsea Hotel*, Simon & Schuster, London, 2014

Ronald B. Tobias, *20 Master Plots and How to Build Them* (second edition), Writer's Digest Books, New York, 2012

Jacob Tomsky, *Heads In Beds: A Reckless Memoir of Hotels, Hustles and So-Called Hospitality*, Anchor Books, New York, 2013

Santi Triviño, *Hotel Dream Rooms: New Interiors Experience*, Monsa, Barcelona, 2012

Nancy J. Troy, *The Afterlife of Piet Mondrian*, University of Chicago Press, Chicago, 2013

Byron Turk (dir.), *The Haunting of Bates Hotel*, New Horizon Films, 2012 (film)

Dana Vachon, 'To Capture Claridge's', *Vanity Fair*, August 2014

Peter Venison, *100 Tips for Hoteliers: What Every Successful Hotel Professional Needs to Know and Do*, iUniverse, New York, 2005

Robin Vousden and Ealan Wingate, *Howard Hodgkin*, Gagosian, Paris, 2014

Ian Wallace, *The Complete A to Z Dictionary of Dreams*, Vermilion, London, 2014

Mark Watson, *Hotel Alpha*, Picador, London, 2014

Evelyn Waugh, *Brideshead Revisited*, Chapman & Hall, London, 1945

—, *Scoop*, Chapman & Hall, London, 1938

David Weaver (dir.), *Century Hotel*, Platinum Disc, 2004 (film)

Wim Wenders (dir.), *The Million Dollar Hotel*, Icon Home Entertainment, 2008 (film)

Geoffrey Wheatcroft, *Yo, Blair!*, Politico's Publishing, London, 2007

Virginia Woolf, *A Room of One's Own*, Hogarth Press, London, 1929

Zhang Yimou (dir.), *Happy Times Hotel*, Twentieth Century Fox, 2002 (film)

Index of Names

Published in 2015 by **Ridinghouse**

46 Lexington Street
London W1F 0LP
United Kingdom
ridinghouse.co.uk

Distributed in the UK and Europe by
Cornerhouse
70 Oxford Street
Manchester M1 5NH
United Kingdom
cornerhouse.org

Distributed in the US by
RAM Publications + Distribution, Inc.
2525 Michigan Avenue Building A2
Santa Monica, CA 90404
United States
rampub.com

Ridinghouse Publisher: Doro Globus
Publishing Manager: Louisa Green
Publishing Assistant: Daniel Griffiths

ISBN 978 1 909932 02 9

British Library Cataloguing-in-
Publication Data: A full catalogue
record of this book is available from
the British Library.

Sold to benefit The Oracle Cancer
Trust: oraclecancertrust.org

Text © Karsten Schubert
For the book in this form
© Ridinghouse

Proofread by Steve Cox
and Karen Kelly
Designed by Tim Harvey
Set in Palatino
Printed in Italy by Studio Fasoli

Special thanks to Gillian Stern